The Gods of Women Have Gone Mad

Wole Akosile

Publisher: Inspiring Publishers,
P.O. Box 159, Calwell, ACT Australia 2905
Email: publishaspg@gmail.com
http://www.inspiringpublishers.com

A catalogue record for this book is available from the National Library of Australia

National Library of Australia Cataloguing-in-Publication entry

Author: Wole Akosile
Title: The Gods of Women Have Gone Mad
Genre: Narrative Fiction
ISBN: 978-0-6483262-6-7

Acknowledgements

To my twin flame, Seyi, thanks for the unwavering support.

To my mother, Folake, thanks for the lessons.

Contents

Chapter 1

Living on My Own Terms

It was a hot, dry afternoon at the top of Bungi Hill. Lami dressed ostentatiously for this dark and liberating act. She had taken time to prepare. The old woman at the village square had colour- synchronized these beads, which now lit up her neck, with the larger ones on her wrists. The whitewashed beads on her ankles and around her calabash-shaped hips glowed in the sun. Multicoloured shells adorned her hair plaited at the village salon the night before. All these adornments beautifully contrasted against her skin.

She was a sight to behold, majestic and sensual as the baubles on her hips swayed with every step she took. She was the epitome of a grown, beautiful young woman in her prime—with those large breasts, her white teeth a perfect contrast to her glowing brown skin.

It was a beautiful day, with clear skies and the sun streaming down through the scattered clouds. The dry season was around the corner, falling leaves creating a beautiful grass carpet. The sun's rays filtered through the scant leaves on the trees.

"Today, I would live on my own terms," she muttered.

Regal but with an ominous air about her, she appeared flustered and indecisive about her next move—this could have an impact on her legacy. The ultimate sacrifice—a virgin sacrifice? A weighty gesture of eternal consequence.

The village will have to perform cleansing rituals. Being dead and deflowered, however, will be the ultimate insult. Pleasure first, pain to follow.

Like a choreographed ritual, she swung her oiled hands in the air. Resting her heart-shaped buttocks against her chosen tree, she parted her wrapper and thrust her fingers high up her thighs. Her eyes closed, she began to perspire as her fingers went in and out in a sort of rhythm.

The sun's brightness intensified as it pierced through the clouds. Hot breeze wheezed across her face as her breathing quickened. The tiny droplets of sweat on her face began trickling down her neck, her bosom, skirting past her navel, down into her pleasure spot. Her fingers continued to engage frantically, almost hysterically. The tree began to shake, dry leaves falling to the ground along with a few dead fruits. Still, she pushed her fingers deeper and faster, making her ecstatic with agony and desire. Blood and sweat lazily trickled down her thighs to her heels, staining her wrapper. She showed no hint of discomfort as the pleasure drowned the pain.

During the morning conversations at the stream, young ladies whispered of self-gratifying sensual acts. This was a taboo, but she revelled in the pleasure unimagined, unhinged. It was like heaven on earth. She found it difficult to articulate the profundity of the pleasure. Her fingers strayed, massaging her firm paw-paw-shaped breasts. Letting out a soft moan, Lami started to breathe faster. Her eyes closed, she smiled, thankful to the loathsome gods. She will miss this one good thing created by the damn gods. Blood and sweat trickled down her thighs and she wiped her bloodstained hands on her wrapper.

She glimpsed the noose on the tree, which she had put there days earlier. It was as she had placed it. It was a difficult decision, but she would have it no other way. Rather than follow the council's decision, she chose death as solace. It was an ash-coloured noose with a large spherical rock underneath it.

She paused, tears trickling down her eyes as she glanced at her place of birth. She saw the brown thatched roofs of huts scattered across the landscape. Young girls darted off to the stream and the luscious green cassava plantation. Lami fought to block the memories of her childhood, remembering how she and the other young girls in the village followed the worn path to the stream. This was their source of clean water. They had a spring in their step on the way to the stream.

A sense of nostalgia filled her as she, unbidden, reminisced about the laughter and games they played there. The stream was a place where girls could be girls away from the prying eyes of the boys in the village. It was an opportunity to exchange ideas, a time to have intellectual discussions on contemporary issues within the community. The stream was a place that gave them a voice, a place of liberty. All young girls looked forward to the daily walk to the stream.

Memories of the days spent by the stream made her chuckle. Her thoughts drifted to her family. What would her mother be doing at this moment? Preparing to go visit her friend, of course. What would her mother do when she does not return? Would Mama cry inconsolably, puzzled, fearing the worst? Ending her life is a drastic action, a bad omen! Lajara, her sister, would curse her for being so defiant.

She smiled to herself. It was a weird and painful smile as tears and sweat began to soak her breasts. Thoughts turned to her father, who would be so ashamed of her decision. Too painful to consider how he would feel, she thought. With resolute defiance, she reached and gripped the rope, whispering,

"Lami, it's time."

Lami climbed the rock, placing the noose around her neck. She squinted at the sun's unrelenting rays. Her fingers were slippery with sweat. For a brief moment, she thought the evening would have been a better time for this. She immediately pushed that thought aside because the evening was a busy time of the day in Rolami. There would be scores of busybodies around. This place would be in full view of the village square. The old women would be entertaining the children with stories. The men would gather under trees in small groups waiting for the call for dinner. No, this was the best time.

With her renewed resolve, she suddenly felt a deafening silence, which lasted for only a moment. Memories started flashing through her mind, such as an argument she'd had with her mother two nights before. It was so vivid. She had yelled, "This will happen over my dead body."

And her mother had stated in a measured tone,

"It's tradition. We all experienced it, and so will you, my dear, you are no different from any of us."

Her sister Lajara's voice whistled loudly in her head.

"If you do this and bring shame and dishonour to our father, sister, I will never forgive you."

Next was Mudi, her best friend, who flashed through her mind. She remembered two nights ago when he begged her to let him take her to a neighbouring village. He had told her they could become outlaws if they escaped.

"I will protect you, Lami, but you need to trust me. You can't do it alone."

Hearing his baritone voice in her head made her heart skip a beat.

It all became quiet again, her heart beating faster, as the cloud covered the sun. There was respite as the breeze became cooler. The perfect signal, she thought.

Lami! Lami! Lami! The sound of her name being called startled her. Was this the first step into oblivion? Was she hearing the voices of her long-passed relatives, welcoming her to the other side? She thought it sounded like her late grandmother. There was a brief pause. *Lami! Lami!* It was louder this time. That did not sound like her grandmother, at all. Is her plot undone? The rapid footsteps became louder. She could make out a familiar voice calling her name. She looked around furiously, thinking her plan had unraveled. "I should have chosen another time," she thought angrily.

She had spent lots of time planning. She had no choice but to make the move today. The council had vetoed her appeal last night and she had three days to act. She had to act immediately. She did not envisage a close monitoring of her movements. She could see young warriors climbing the hill in her direction. When she finally saw them coming, she awkwardly tilted her body forward, the noose choking her, robbing the light from her eyes. The blackness was instantaneous.

Chapter 2

The Cleansing

November in Rolami was dry season—a time for clear skies and parched soil. Trees were at the tail-end of shedding their leaves. The rays of the sun were unrelenting during the day, while evenings were a time of solace with the cool breeze caressing people's sweaty faces. Despite the dryness, some rugged crops thrived. The dryness made everything dusty.

Dark brown huts contrasted with light-coloured straw roofs interspersed along the road. Dust hung in the air and settled everywhere. Barely clothed children ran across the streets, covered with dust as they played. Young boys played football, their usual pastime. Those who didn't make the team gathered round to watch with their brown clay-smeared faces from playing rough in the mud, hoping to make the next team. A fresh breeze carried the scent of roasted plantain and corn, which pervaded the air. Old men sat on stools around the charcoal pot, watching the corncobs sizzle in the heat. The old men laughed and chatted while they drank *brukutu,* the local alcoholic drink brewed from guinea corn and millet. Their eyes ogled the young women. The notorious womanizer Buzu tapped the lady roasting her wares on the rump. She squirmed at his unsolicited gesture.

The farmlands were like a collage, with sections gradually shifting from brown to light green. Few crops had the capacity to withstand the intensity of the sun and still flourish. The farmers moved like tiny specks of brown dots across the fields, their chatter and clatter like a broken symphony. Men and women attended to their business.

Amidst the mild chaos, you could intuit the shimmering sound of the dry thatch as it had become hotter.

The mood became more sombre. A group of enthusiastic street urchins walked from the base of Bungi Hill, marching through the dusty roads of the village in the heat. Chaos followed them. They shoved aside young girls carrying their wares, scattering them on the wayside. The fierce-looking warriors carried a beautiful brown- skinned lady on their shoulders. She offered little or no resistance. She wore the traditional ceremonial dress worn only for special occasions, which was odd as there was no announced feast, festival or ceremony.

Women exchanged curious glances as they performed their chores, pretending to be busy while trying to understand what was going on. They wondered what event attempted to colour what would have been an ordinary day. Each tried to take in as much detail as possible while attempting to appear disinterested and dignified. They wanted information, so they could supply the salacious details at the evening rendezvous at the stream. Some yet unable to contain themselves ran to join the group, struggling to catch a glimpse of the lady. People asked in raised voices:

"What is happening?" "Is someone in trouble?"

"She must have been trying to elope with a man from a forbidden tribe."

Others smacked their hands together in excitement, gesturing toward the warriors. The whispers and murmurs got louder as the crowd grew. Teenage boys climbed trees, jumping as high as they could. Some stood on top of one another to catch a glimpse.

The lady's traditional wrapper was bloodstained and she had ligature marks on her neck. Fish-eyed warriors walked with swift steps. The custodians, the women who performed the ritual, followed. They were four frail, elderly women with deep reflective eyes that belied their age. You could sense anger from their demeanor, but they could not hide the ecstatic grin on their faces.

They've got her. The voluble Lami, who had been a thorn in their flesh. This was a day they had anticipated for a long time. The conclave of elders only delayed the inevitable. This was victory for "tradition."

The custodians were dressed in their ceremonial white wrappers tied across their chests, with a red scarf knotted above their waists. The first custodian was burning incense, while the other two were muttering incantations. The paramount custodian was Haditha who towered above the rest. She walked with a hunched back and suffered from titubation. Haditha masticated her chewing stick and spat at will.

The village revered Haditha. In her heyday, men had to raise their heads to speak to her because she was so tall. According to folklore, her height was the reason the gods had made her lead custodian. Custodians never married and do not have offspring. Custom had it that every girl child born in the village was the daughter of the custodian by proxy. Haditha always had a strange glowing grin whenever it was time for this ceremony. The ceremony that freaked out most of the young ladies.

Some lost interest the moment they recognised the young lady hoisted on the warriors' shoulders. The emotions were mixed within the increasing crowd. Most noticeable was the young ladies present. Their excitement and curiosity turned into horror the moment they recognised her. Some even began to cry and wail while others walked away with their heads downcast. This was a disaster. All their hopes dashed by this singular imagery unfolding before them.

The beautiful lady in ceremonial dress was Lami, the outspoken daughter of the respected village mediator and scribe, Magda. She had been vocal in her defiance of the circumcision ritual. It was the norm, a rarely questioned tradition, until Lami started to talk about it. Her speeches at the stream had given the other young women a new perspective. They had dared to dream, dared to hope things could change. She had tried to change the status quo. Alas! While there was nothing unusual about the ceremony itself, the person in question today made it something out of the ordinary. She had been defiant to this tradition.

Lami was finally taken into the circumcision hut, called by the villagers as a "place of transition," which towered above most of the huts in the village. Its inner walls were painted with white dye, with one large window located in its eastern part. The window had a mesh made from dyed straw woven by assistants of the custodians. The primary responsibility of the assistants was to see to the general maintenance of the hut. The single window and door were the only source of natural light into the hut, which had little by way of furnishings. In the centre was an elevated slab made from baked mud similar in height to the table used at the council. Each corner of the slab was fitted with a small pole and a firm string designed to restrain their victim.

Lami was placed on the slab, on her back, with her wrists tied to it. Straight-faced men who had brought her in took their leave at this stage to guard the hut. They stopped any nosy person from entering the hut while the ceremony took place.

It was taboo for men to partake in the sacred ceremony. Rolami is a patriarchal society, in which men played a preeminent role in every aspect except circumcision. A man's presence in this ceremony invoked a curse on his family.

The assistant elevated her knees and tied her legs to the slab with the string. All was set for the ceremony. They made incantations inviting the spirits to bless the ceremony. They poured libations, requesting the gods be with the custodians, to grant them wisdom and ensure a smooth transition for Lami. A custodian proceeded to mark Lami's face with white chalk to prepare her for the transition. This turned out chaotic and then was abandoned. Lami struggled defiantly, waving her head and trying to bite them.

Haditha gave orders for the ritual to begin.

"We will do this with or without the face painting today," she said in a low tone, gritting her teeth. The gravity of what was about to take place dawned on Lami. She began begging for mercy, but the loud incantations drowned out her voice.

Haditha lit the lanterns in the four corners of the room. As the room became brighter, the more eerie she felt. Shadows rose and fell as the soft breeze fanned the lanterns' flames. The shadows created images as though there was a crowd of several women littering the tiny room. Haditha lit the final and biggest lantern and placed it on the slab itself, illuminating the room. She edged close to Lami and, in her low-pitched hoarse voice reputed to scare even the dead, muttered,

"We were going to do this with or without your consent. It will save you from being a whore in this life and in the afterlife."

She paused and pinched Lami's earlobes so that Lami looked at her.

"You are a disgrace to us and to your family," Haditha said. "See the shameful way your transition has turned out.

There should have been music and dancing. Your friends waiting at the door to escort you home once your transition is complete. Your family would have thrown a party today. The elders would have gathered in your father's compound to congratulate him. Your mother should have been proud today, because it is your day of transition. She would have bought a new wrapper and adorned herself for the occasion. She would have been the envy of the women whose daughters are yet to reach the age of transition. She would have been dancing with her friends to the market square, handing out white handkerchiefs to young girls. You would have been the envy of the young girls who would soon meet the age of transition. Instead, you bring shame to your family and to our village. You dare defy our traditions!"

She spat on the floor in disgust and anger, then walked around the table while the others continued with the incantations. One of them started brandishing the ceremonial knives, which glistened and made a slashing sound. She then set out the knives in order on the slab as was the custom.

Lami was in a state of extreme apprehension. Her eyes, hawk-like, followed Haditha's movements. She trembled, knowing what was to follow. The illumination of the room and the banishing apparatus did not help matters at all. At this stage, she was trembling. She kept blaming herself for wasting time. Had she been quicker she would have ended her life and would not be in this position. Every young girl from Rolami would have seen her as a martyr. That's not possible now.

She bit her lip to fight back the tears, as she did not want to appear weak before Haditha. Haditha leaned over her, her breath reeking of garlic, her frail figure looking puffed up. She barked down at Lami, showering her with garlic-flavoured spittle.

"You know what they say, the goat that wants to go missing will forget the sound of the shepherd's whistle. We warned you several times but you remained defiant. I will carve this day into your memory forever. Whenever a man touches you, you will relive it, my words will spring from the dead to hunt you!"

Haditha picked up the knife designed for the ritual. It was extremely sharp. In that moment, she looked like a skilled psychopathic surgeon with her team. Haditha hissed as she prepared to work, going through the tools wrapped in a clean white cloth.

The other custodians set out to work, holding a piece of cloth over Lami's nose. This cloth was soaked in a traditional liquid designed to help make the passage easier. Lami, after a few breaths, felt euphoric and her body relaxed. Two other custodians held her knees apart for Haditha to perform the ritual.

None of the custodians seemed to show any sympathy. If indeed they felt empathy toward her, they hid their emotions quite well. They conducted themselves in an unvarnished manner, fulfilling the motions. Who could blame them? They did this for every daughter of Rolami. They had done this since the oracle named them custodians in the prime of their youth.

Some of the villagers had gathered outside the hut. They tried to watch the event, whispering amongst themselves, each wanting to see everything unfold firsthand. Some considered it a gruesome event, man's most wicked act to a woman. The men at the entrance kept them at a distance. No one could interrupt the ritual.

Haditha took the knife and in a low piercing voice said to Lami,

"Look at me!"

Lami closed her eyes. She was sweating even though the hut was cool despite the intensity of the sun outside. The slab was drenched with her sweat. Haditha poked Lami a few times, asking her to look at her.

Nadi, one of the custodians, beckoned to Haditha to get on with it. Nadi was the bearer of the incense, the medium that brought the spirits. Nadi was the shortest and stockiest of all four custodians. She had an obvious ptosis of her left eye. She was a quiet woman who spoke few words and who had actually gone to the stream on many occasions to listen to Lami speak. She'd pondered over Lami's arguments and concluded they were the ramblings of an overindulged brat.

Nadi was the most sympathetic of the custodians. She held the hands of the girls going through the transition ritual in an attempt to make them feel better. Her kind gesture didn't go unnoticed by the women in the village. After the ceremony, the mothers of the transitioned ladies sent bowls of food to Nadi. This was at the request of their daughters.

On this occasion, she did not attempt to hold Lami's hand. She did not want to risk getting into Haditha's bad books.

Haditha squirmed at Nadi's sign. She usually became very angry whenever she felt her leadership challenged. She gave her a long hard stare with her eyes rolling up and down in disgust, capping it off with loud disapproving hisses. In one swift motion, as she waved her hands to rebuke Nadi, she parted Lami's legs using her elbow as a lever. She put her thumb and index finger between Lami's thighs and looking surprised she exclaimed,

"You are not a virgin?"

Haditha froze and Lami's facial expression shifted from one of despair to a smile.

She whispered, her tone sounding triumphant,

"How can you save me? I am already possessed by the demon of promiscuity."

Angered and overwhelmed with rage, Haditha moved toward Lami's vagina with the knife. Lami screamed in pain as the transition started. Haditha cut off the clitoris. As Lami's deviant and defiant behavior warranted extra punishment, her labia majora and minora were sliced off with accurate precision.

Lami shook her head wildly, gnashing her teeth. Her head movement made it difficult for the custodian to hold the cloth over her nose. The pain was unbelievable, much worse than she could have imagined. Nadi tried to hold her hands but it provided little comfort. The other custodians cleaned up the wound while completing the last stage of the ritual by pouring libations to the spirits, praying for a successful ritual and smooth transition. The transition was not deemed complete until the wound healed.

Lami and her gang of friends thought the ritual was crude and archaic. They believed it was a pseudo bid to suppress promiscuity. Several times at the stream they proclaimed that it had the opposite effect. It releases girls into an experience they will hardly recover from. They described this ritual as a hideous act based on an evil custom. A foolish value system, a cursed norm passed down by the custodians of a mad system.

Their assertion had angered the custodians for years, particularly Haditha who saw this as a challenge to her position, an attempt to dethrone her as chief custodian. The custodians had waited for this day, savouring vengeance on the ringleader of those who dared to challenge them.

Lami convulsed, feeling unimaginable pain, screaming as she bled. She tightened her grip on the custodians but there was no sympathy in their eyes. Except for Nadi who, although her face was devoid of emotion, stroked her hair to try to calm her down. The other custodians could not help themselves. They exchanged glances and then grinned with joy. As their gazes met, they thought, *it serves the little twat right.*

They untied her and pushed her away with a measure of disdain. She was being treated like a person cursed by the oracle. They wanted to distance themselves and not share in her curse. She coiled up in a corner, weeping without restraint.

"Be quiet!" one of the custodians yelled.

Her punishment was not over. The ritual was not deemed a punishment. Because she had attempted to run away and take her own life, she would be served punishment. She had attempted to commit a taboo. Her punishment had been delayed until the transition was complete.

The custodians and supporters of tradition disliked her with a passion. To them, she must be punished heavily. This would be a deterrent for other young girls. The punishment was also to serve as a form of spiritual cleansing. The cane was the antidote to youthful folly. The custodians and traditionalists believed this ceremony prevented promiscuity. The gods ordained it to stop the activity of the demon of youth in women.

Lami believed it was all a farce. She had concluded a long time ago that the circumcised would never find true pleasure. How then would promiscuity stop? Despite the decades of circumcision, promiscuity still existed and was rife.

Now she was going through unimaginable pain. She knew she was also going to receive a public flogging to act as a deterrent to others. As she wept in a corner, dejected, without strength, Lami squeezed her hands between her legs to prevent further bleeding. All that mattered to her at this point was the disgrace she had brought on her father, a respected chief in the village. He would disown her and her mother would feel shame without end.

The custodians' assistant covered her with a big wrapper. They then pulled open the door of the hut, shoving her out in the open. She stumbled on her feet, too weak to offer any further resistance. She walked carefully, awkwardly, to minimize the pain. She was a spectacle of ignominy before all the young girls. They had put on notice her gang of so-called enlightened women. They can behold their symbol of pain and totem of folly, Lami! All who see her will be certain that the gods were not fooling around. Not a single girl will escape this rite of passage no matter how noble their lineage, no matter how enlightened they think they were.

She cried, feeling deflated, as the physical pain was much but the emotional torture was worse. She felt like a failure. She had failed future generations. She stood outside the hut with her head downcast, unable to bring herself to look into the eyes of those who had gathered outside the hut. She could sense murmuring. Out of the corner of her eyes, she could see the teeming mottled crowd of people of all ages, all colours, their faces bearing judgment. Some spoke among themselves, some grinning, some with their mouths hanging open. Others were catatonic and terrified at the identity of the recipient of such embarrassment. A few were sympathetic.

Those who had seen many harvests only watched with disinterest. They had seen it all before. More valiant women with royal blood who had fallen. They had tried to resist the female circumcision ritual without success. Many of these previous mutineers had turned into radical protagonists of the old culture.

"Lami! Lami!" She heard her name in that familiar baritone voice. A young man pushed through the surging crowd, only to be stopped in his tracks by the men guarding

the ritual hut and its grounds. A little scuffle ensued, drawing the attention of Haditha.

The young man stood six feet tall, a well-sculptured man with lean muscles, featuring a distinct scar on his forehead that extended to his left cheek. He exuded a distinguished bearing, with many healed keloid scars on his back from floggings he had experienced during his initiation into adulthood.

This was Mudi, Lami's best friend. He was at this point pinned to the ground by three of the warriors. He came with three older women who were kneeling and begging for mercy. Their voices towered above the murmuring and whispering of the crowd. Some women in the crowd also joined them to ask for mercy on behalf of Lami.

Haditha looked up to see what was causing the commotion.

She recognized him and shook her head in disgust and roared,

"Mudi! Mudi! Do you seek trouble? Do you not know she is an offender? And you show such gesture of kindness?"

"She has suffered enough,"

he grunted, despite the elbow against his throat.

"I plead with my mothers, waive the flogging, please."

Silence descended. Even Lami stopped sobbing. Haditha glanced at the whole scene. The women on their knees begging for mercy on behalf of Lami, the long and sad faces looking at Haditha with facial expressions doing the same. She took a brief glance at the other custodians and Nadi nodded. Haditha asked the men to free him, who then reluctantly obeyed, with Mudi still pushing and shoving.

"Take her out of my sight, and you, Mudi, must see me later."

He only nodded as three of the women on their knees supported Lami, who was spared from the shame of a public flogging. Knowing Haditha, no one expected that. Haditha had a soft spot for Mudi.

They covered her from head to toe with a large white wrapper, as though preparing her for burial. It was clear in her mind that ignominy and dishonour had latched on to her. This event would haunt her all her life. All eyes were on them as she left with Mudi and the women that accompanied him.

Chapter 3

Post-circumcision Blues

The morning trip to the river at Rolami was an integral part of life. It started in the wee hours of the morning, at the crack of dawn. As the roosters' crow cut through the quiet stillness, the young girls got up from their mats and picked up their water pots.

The long winding road to the river entertained many travellers. Young ladies picked each other up along the way. In no time, as they formed into different groups of friends, the loud chatter began. The young mothers had their suckling babies strapped to their backs.

It was a long trek, but no one minded. It was the perfect opportunity to exchange and fill up on the latest gossip. For the married, it was a time of solace away from an overbearing Rolami man. Some did not fall into any group and walked alone in quiet meditation.

The air was clean and fresh and the birds had only started to stir. The sun was waking up. It was the best time of the day for many girls in Rolami. They would spend time gossiping and also have a swim in the river before returning home. The path to the river was either dusty or muddy depending on the time of year. While they walked through the village the different groups were quiet. They would walk through the road networks linking several huts so as not to wake the men. This was only until they passed the hut of Birinkin at the outskirts.

Lami's mother, Hajaru, and Mudi's mother, Mematha, were best friends. Hajaru was a tall, slim woman with a long, pale, oval face, full bow-shaped lips and a long slender neck. She had small perky breasts which belied years of breast-feeding. Her full hips had a gentle sensual touch about them. Her light-brown skin was surprisingly smooth. She was soft-spoken and had an irresistible smile.

She was the only wife of the village scribe, Magda, which was rare in a place where chiefs had many wives. It was generally uncommon for middle-aged men in the village to have only one wife. As men became more comfortable they took on another wife. It was a common saying among the men that Magda had begged the gods for a beautiful wife. In exchange, he must not look elsewhere for comfort on all the days numbered for him on this earth.

In contrast, Mematha was short and well-rounded. She was a slim lady when she got married but had filled out over the years. Unlike her friend, she was the first of the many wives of Buzu, her husband, a prominent chief and popular shaman.

Buzu's adventures with women had become legendary at so- called *brukutu* joints. There were many scandals linked to his name. He was a notorious womaniser, yet his behaviour was somewhat condoned in Rolami because of his high status.

As a shaman, Buzu specialized in making love potions. Many young women flocked to him seeking potions to make a desired man fall in love with them. He often told his customers to try out the magic potion on himself first to test its potency. Many of those women agreed and became among his many wives. His residential compound was the busiest in the village. It was almost as busy as the village market square, booming with wives and children.

It was often said that Buzu did not know how many children he actually fathered, as he was also notorious for climbing into other men's beds. So only the gods know how many children he actually had. Proud of his escapades, he gave himself the moniker, "the three-legged animal." The man who stood on a tripod (because of the purported length of his penis).

In Buzu's world, sex could fix anything, and every woman's problem was the result of inadequate sex. He'd tell young men who came to him with relationship problems that sex could be a punishment or reward. Buzu could be gregarious and at times behaved like a buffoon.

He was a conservative icon. He stood for the status quo when it came to customs and tradition. He would not hear of any attempt to change any custom or tradition. He opposed anyone who attempted to bring any change to age-old customs. He would not even listen to whatever they had to say. He was adored by many even though he was a tyrant within his home.

Hajaru and Mematha's children, Lami and Mudi, were the best of friends. Because of the closeness of their mothers, they had grown up together. Mematha spent a great deal of time in Hajaru's home. She found it a refuge from the organized chaos in Buzu's compound. She was always settling quarrels among the younger wives or their children. As the first wife of Buzu, Mematha wielded some level of influence in the compound. She loved spending time with Hajaru and especially enjoyed being in her home. It was a time for her to reflect.

Hajaru and Mematha also loved gardening. Over the years, they built a decent garden at the corner of Magda's compound. They grew some flowers and vegetables. They gave the garden so much attention. The vegetables were so lovely, becoming a village treasure. They gave the fruits of the garden as gifts. Whenever a woman had a new baby in the village she was sure to receive a basket of vegetables from the famous garden. New mothers looked forward to a gift from the garden. They were both proud of their garden as it held a special place in their hearts. It was their little sanctuary to which both women retreated. Lami and Mudi had also grown up in and around the garden. It was there where Lami took her first steps.

Mudi was like a strong wild ox, a restless soul, impulsive and brutish at times. He was well known to never turn down a fight. He had a good heart, a strong sense of injustice. He was the spitting image of his father. He had strong facial features, a big nose, a square jaw and large eyes.

He had carved a niche for himself from an early age as a ladies' man, but in a different way from his father. He was quick to leap to the defence of young girls bullied by older boys on the walk to the river. He'd had a few teeth knocked out in the process. He'd never back down, fighting until he'd wear down his opponents.

The young ladies felt safe whenever he was around. He was also a social reformer of some sort, speaking against perceived injustice in the community. Young men looked up to him and loved being under his wings.

Mudi grew up watching Buzu assault all his wives, including his mother. On the other hand, he also observed how Magda never raised so much as a finger against his "second" mother, Hajaru. As he grew older, he began to resent his father. He did not like his father's reputation when it came to women and felt that his father belittled women. He also could not stand how his father assaulted his mother. He had observed the other men who had more than one wife and noted that most did not assault their wives.

He spoke against domestic violence against women. He had stood up for his mother a few times and endured beating at the hands of Buzu. The beatings of his mother became fewer over the years as she grew older, as Buzu had younger wives to harass and keep in line.

Mudi also, on some occasion, would stand up to his father on behalf of some of the other women in the compound. When Mudi became a man, Buzu realized he could no longer hit his son or he would be doing so at his own peril. There were now two lions in the pride: one a dishonourable aging brute and the other a young, strong heir filled with hatred and resentment for his elder.

Mudi had become a bull with horns ready to charge down any perceived threat from Buzu. Mudi would stand up to anyone who attempted to assault any of his half-sisters, but the "aging lion" seemed to always have the last laugh, as he wielded enormous influence in the community.

The girls went to extreme lengths to get Mudi's attention, each hoping he would choose them as his bride. He was an eligible bachelor given his rugged good looks and his family status. Mudi, however, did not seem to notice any of the advances from women. His attention was focused on his soul mate, Lami. He would do anything for her. He wanted her to be his bride, to marry her and live with her forever.

He loved the fact that Lami spoke her mind and was not intimidated by anyone. He could not imagine being a husband to a woman who considered herself her husband's property. He did not conform to the village norms, and neither did Lami, and he loved her for that.

Lami, although shorter than Mudi, was the spitting image of her mother. She was so beautiful, with her round, curvaceous hips; with the way she stood like a tall black Amazon princess, a paragon of beauty. Lami was the prettiest damsel in Rolami in Mudi's mind. Even as a young girl, Lami possessed a vigorous intellect, incessantly throwing her parents questions about anything under the sun. "Why should Papa get the largest meat? Is it because he is a boy?"

Her father, Magda, loved her so much. They spent hours together daily when she was younger. He patiently answered all her questions. Whenever she was not in the garden with her mother she was with her father.

Magda was from the great lineage of herdsmen, so his family was nomadic. He often told his children nostalgic stories of his life as a herdsman, the adventures he had with his brothers when he was younger. He remembered the day a messenger arrived in his father's compound. He noticed his father's nervous expression at the sight of the messenger. His father invited the messenger into his hut. A short while later they summoned his mother to his father's hut. The messenger then left.

Later in the evening, the news was broken: a distant relative who he only knew as the village scribe had passed away. He wondered why the news had to be delivered in person. His father went on to say that the relative did not have a male heir to succeed him as the scribe. The oracle had chosen Magda to succeed him as scribe.

Magda had to proceed to Rolami immediately. He would learn the customs for one full harvest from the elite school of scribes, after which he would take the oath and become the scribe.

Mudi and Lami grew up chasing each other on the riverside, climbing hills, bathing in the waters. Lami was fair-skinned with bright brown eyes. Until the age of four, she ran around with the darker and older Mudi. They loved each other. Their contrasting skin tones were distinct and enthralling. Many of their friends wished their fairy-tale relationship would end in marriage. Most families betrothed their girls as wives from a young age to men who were much older than them. It was rare for a girl to have a say in who would become her husband.

Quite often, most girls marry early. Their prospective husbands usually came knocking as soon as they felt she was old enough. Most young men could not afford the dowry and costs associated with marriage. A girl within their age group was generally out of reach.

There was no limit to what parents could ask for as dowry, the great "compensation" for raising girls. The established middle-aged men got all the young, beautiful girls. Mudi and his group of radical young men had started to agitate for change. They considered this custom a dead one that had refused to change with the times. The young men thought it was unrealistic but their views began to change as they grew grey hair.

Today's walk to the river was difficult and slow. Different thoughts raced through Mudi's mind. These were only interrupted by grunts and occasional screams from Lami. He knew Lami had a high pain threshold. This kind of pain was virgin territory even for her. She was unable to walk and leaned heavily on the women supporting her.

Mudi walked behind them, gathering some herbs as they walked. Today he was not able to appreciate the scenery. Most of the trees and shrubs had shed their leaves. Now they stood bare against the backdrop of the sun. The landscape was softened by the blue flowers of the migun tree, which only flowered in the dry season. This picturesque background was a complete contrast to their reality at present.

When they arrived at the river, Mudi asked the women to clean up Lami and cover her with a clean wrapper. Handing over the herbs, he told them how to use them. He had learned about the medicinal herbs for pain from his father. On rare occasions when they went to the bush together, he showed him a few. He had enjoyed those moments when he was a young boy. These became few and far between as Mudi got older and tension with his father grew.

He was stoic in his disposition. His heart had melted with scorching sorrow emanating from its core.

"Things were not supposed to play out this way," he sighed.

He walked some distance from the women. Seeing Lami's naked body before the official family introduction was a taboo. The women took Lami farther up the river to a secluded part.

Mudi asked everyone to vacate the stream. Everyone obeyed. Mudi was the son of a chief. A popular warrior leading young men to defend the city against neighbours from the north. They murmured and whispered as they dispersed.

Mudi stroked his facial scar; his heart was racing and his throat was parched and dry. The sound of the moving river deepened his thirst. He was sweating profusely from his nose and forehead, moisture trickling down the angle of his mouth, finding his taste buds and kissing it with its saltiness. He rubbed his eyes drenched with his brackish sweat.

A persistent nuisance to his ears were the buzzing houseflies. They reminded him that otherwise, it was just another day at the stream.

Her screams were like a dagger to his heart. He would peep whenever she let out a particularly loud scream, visualizing tears running down her pretty eyes, like a rushing stream.

"Why, Lami, why?"

He whispered under his breath. Tears dropped from Mudi's eyes, and he could not hold them back. There was a saying in these parts: "Men can cry but not more than women." He was a man overwhelmed with grief and anger.

The gods had been merciful and there was no one else at the river. The crowd had not followed her to the river to please their curiosity. He could express his emotions in private. The women were too busy with Lami to notice his tears.

The women begged her not to cry, their soft tones bringing little or no comfort to their "patient." They had carried her and placed her close to the riverbank. They encouraged her to spread her legs apart. She screamed as she attempted to do so. The pain was unimaginable. She wished she were dead and would wake up to discover it was a bad dream. The women used the local herbs to clean the outer part of her vagina as Mudi had instructed. She screamed, her whole body vibrating from the pain.

It was a period of pain and anguish, lasting only a few minutes, but it seemed like forever. He clenched his fist, unsure of who should be the recipient of his anger. Could he dare to be angry at the gods? Who breaches the law of the gods? Their anger lasts forever.

Could they unleash untold hardship on himself and his family? Are the custodians dense? They were literal and thoughtless in their interpretation of the laws, refusing to consider that some aspects of the law could be symbolic.

Lami, the woman who was as stubborn as a goat, defiant, refusing to conform to tradition. The cocky peacock, he thought. She has brought shame and notoriety upon herself, her family and their relationship. When the women had finished, they came to him, excused themselves and left.

Lami thanked the women as they retreated. There was an awkward silence that seemed to last for eternity. Lami looked to the ground downcast, her shoulders slumped. She looked like a shadow of herself. She raised her head to see what Mudi was doing. The spark in her eyes was gone. The pride that oozed from her being had dissipated. She looked like she had added decades to her age. It was a sorry sight.

There was no sound and it was almost as if even the plants stood still. The only sound was that of the moving river. Their eyes met as Lami lifted her head, their gazes locking for a few moments that felt like an eternity. Mudi's eyes softened. He reached out and lifted her off her feet and stroked her passionately to ease the pain. No words were spoken. The silence was punctuated only by the moving river and indolent flies that buzzed in their ears.

For some reason, they could not look into each other's eyes. Mudi found it surprising that he had mixed emotions. He was not sure whether to be empathetic, angry or indifferent. Indifference left his mind blank, and this made him feel better.

The intensity of the sun increased and they were both sweating, unable to calm the turbulent waves of questions running through his mind. This was worsened by the uncomfortable silence. Suddenly, he blurted out,

"Why? Why did you run?"

Scared to give an answer to the love of her life, she looked even farther away from him. She arched her spine, stiffened her long brown legs and stretched out her body. She winced as the pain between her legs intensified.

He asked again, his voice louder and more impatient. Pulling her shoulders toward him as if reminding her that he'd asked a question. He wanted an answer, his eyes demanded it. He tightened his grip—there was nothing tender about the grip. She felt uncomfortable.

"Why did you run? Why?"

He gazed deeply into her eyes. For the first time, he could not read her emotion. Her usually expressive eyes were now blank, seemingly devoid of anything. It hurt him to see her like this but he needed to know what pushed her to do what she did. Did she not trust him to protect her?

She remained silent for a few more minutes. She turned away from him, her gaze finding the horizon far away. She said,

"You know why I did it, don't you?"

"Those urban nurses have influenced you. Those who fuck around with the locals have told you lies," barked Mudi. He hissed, shaking his head in disbelief.

"They are not lies," she snapped.

"It is real, and it is true. Once circumcised you lose the ability to enjoy sex."

Mudi, feeling exasperated, asked pointedly,

"How in the world do you know this? Are you having affairs behind my back?"

He pushed her to the side and for the first time they looked into each other's eyes. Lami hissed and laughed sarcastically.

"Affairs? Mudi, the son of Buzu, asks if I am having affairs?"

She clapped her hands in disgust, pushing him backward. As she did so, she recoiled, feeling a sharp pain between her legs. She winced as she tried to sit up.

"Have the tale bearers whispered? Have they concocted tales by moonlight? Tales borne by the wings of busybodies served to their customers with itchy ears. Their hot gossip passing from one secret place to another. Otherwise, who will buy it? Did they mention a few who have played down there?" She pointed between her legs.

"Are they big and strong, like Mudi, my one true prince?" She laughed sardonically.

"Oh wait, if they have been there before, they will not recognize it anymore."

With tears trickling down her cheeks she continued,

"It's now like a city pillaged by wicked hunters without mercy. Everything destroyed in its wake. And then you ask me, have I been having affairs? Pleasure comes with or without the privilege of a man. A woman must know her body in and out, it's hers and hers alone until she chooses to share it with another. In my darkest moment, I realized this one truth. I greased the entrance to this eternal well, I felt a joy that I have not felt before. I cannot find words to explain the rushing gust of pure pleasure. It was better than a thousand embraces combined."

Lami continued sobbing, her voice hoarse from the pain. "I need no one to enjoy this lovely treasured nectar of the gods. This pleasure is taken from me. This unhealthy, messed-up, wicked ritual of circumcision has stolen my key to happiness."

"You call the culture of our fathers messed up?!" Mudi yelled.

"You call the norms we have passed from one generation to the next wicked? Must we not restrain the profanity of a woman? Must we not restrain the demon in her that makes her jump from one man's bed to another? Causing men to fight, clans to clash, blood to spill. Must we not? Who caused the war between the Gwojes and Turans? Who caused the clan cleansing in the north? Was it not a woman? Answer me."

He held her and shook her, forcing her to look at him.

"You ran to the hills, with only the gods knowing where you thought you were going. Are they not everywhere? Does their reach not go far beyond human comprehension? Why should we change traditions as old as our community because some visitor said it is archaic? They have not been to our festivals. They have not observed the ancient wisdom of which your father is the custodian! They dare to label evil what they do not understand and stand aloof passing judgment. Do you go to a man's house and tell him how to conduct his affairs?"

Mudi's voice was shaking with anger; there was fire in his eyes. Lami had never seen him this way. Was he playing devil's advocate?

There was a brief silence. Mudi's countenance turned from anger to anguish. His neck hanging low, his eyes looking away and with more prosody to his tone, he asked,

"I would like to know if this is true. Rumours have it that they found you with a noose around your neck? Tell me it's a lie, Lami! Tell me it's not true!"

Lami said nothing. She looked down and slowly sat on the ground, gazing into the distance.

"Lami, do we not matter? It's all about you, isn't it? We grew up together, it's been five harvests since I expressed my feelings for you. Did you even consider your father, your mother or your sister? You have caused such shame and pain to everyone. All because you are running away from principles laid down by the gods. Principles that have been in existence before you or your father was born. Who told you that you won't enjoy sex? With whom will you have it? Those urban nurses are crazy dogs. They, who are so perverse, yet uncircumcised sleeping around with locals. Don't be a fool, Lami."

"It is all wrong Mudi, it is," Lami snapped.

The tears started to pour again. She picked up a dead branch and plucked the leaves still hanging onto it. There was a brief silence, as she seemed to be contemplating what to say.

"Why do we blame the gods? They are all-knowing and created us as the elders say," she spoke after a while.

"From conception, they have given us all we need to survive in life. Have we stopped to wonder whether or not they would have made us with so many flaws? Or given us body parts that have no use?"

Mudi replied, "I don't know, ask the gods."

Lami rolled her eyes.

"See what happens to all those young girls given early in marriage to those old pigs. Those shameless wizards. Those girls are often not able to hold urine after childbirth. Urinating without control. The same does not happen to girls who get married at an older age. These poor girls, rejected by the same men who bought them with cattle. The same men who made them premature mothers. Did the same fate not befall your sister?"

Mudi clenched his teeth.

"Your sharp, poisonous tongue is unbridled in its movement. It releases untamed stinging words that won't change what has been and what will be. Are you greater than our fathers? From the beginning, they meticulously ensured that every generation experiences our tradition. Without these traditions, we are not a people…"

"Where are the Gwans?" Lami interjected.

"I don't know, Lami. I don't want to hear this. I have heard this story several times. You are only a young woman and you are already repeating your stories like a senile old hag…"

Lami hissed, but she was only getting more spirited.

"Oh no! You will hear this once again. There is only a handful of them left. Why? A century ago there were thousands. They refused to adapt, they refused to change with the times. They forgot that ancient traditions should only remind us of who we were and not who we should be. But the Gabinda people are flourishing. They adapt their culture to the changing times—"

Mudi raised his right hand to his ears and with his left index finger he motioned to her to be quiet.

"…Do you hear my name…?"

She kept quiet and listened. The intensity of the sun was beginning to wane. The sun had shifted on the horizon; it was time for it to retreat after a hard day's work and hand over to its cousin the moon.

It sounded like whispers as the wind's caress changed from hot to cool.

Mudi arched his eyebrows, wondering whether he was hallucinating. He thought he heard his name again. Were the gods playing tricks on him or did he actually hear his name? The breeze lifted some dirt that went into Mudi's eyes. He rubbed them to get the dirt out. He heard his name again, this time it was louder. The sun was setting, and shadows had begun to get longer. He looked around again, placing his hand on his forehead to guide his eyes.

In the distance, he could make out a figure. It was a woman. He squinted so he could get a clear view as he wanted to know who it was. When he recognized her, he almost lost his balance. She was his flesh and blood; he had heard rumours, but he had chosen not to believe them. He had not seen her for a few harvests. He remembered the last time he saw her. It was her wedding day. She had held onto his hands, extremely terrified. When the women indicated it was time to escort her to her husband's house, she did not want to go. He had whispered in her ears,

"You will be fine. The gods will go with you and help you prosper."

She had looked up into his eyes unconvinced as the women led her away. Something about the way she looked at him haunted him to this day. She looked frail, her hair locked and matted. Her skin had lost its dark glow, her perky breasts were flat. Her gait was slow and lopsided, and her curvy hips were a caricature of her once solid frame. Her dirty wrapper belied her status as the wife of a chief. She was one of his many wives, though. Mudi and Lami froze as she approached. She was a shadow of her former self. Her disarming smile reassured them all was well. Both were surprised to see her.

He struggled to mutter,

"Halima!"

The lady was Halima, Mudi's sister. She was cute and petite, with a charming oval face. Her soft angelic smile could soothe the wounded heart, yet she could become ferocious when she perceived malice toward her. As she approached, Mudi remembered how their father Buzu traded her for another woman. Buzu had done this to solidify his political position in Rolami. Buzu was also unhappy with Halima because she mingled with a group of renegade young females (the "enlightened" women). These ladies led by Lami challenged some cultural practices in Rolami. They described these practices as oppressive to women.

At the time, Halima was betrothed to the son of the chief of chiefs and had plans to marry when she turned eighteen. He was only a few years older than her. Buzu called off the engagement. He wanted to punish her. This endeared him further to the conservative stalwarts in Rolami. Buzu had not been in support of the betrothal to a younger man, he only played along. Buzu would not tolerate such in his household.

To solve the problem and keep Halima quiet he decided to hand her over to one of the village chiefs, Isti, as a wife. She was only fourteen when Buzu gave her away to Isti whose grandchildren were older than her. He accepted one of Isti's younger daughters as a wife, who was much older than Halima. Mudi was unhappy about it and this act increased the tension between father and son. It was not uncommon in Rolami for girls to marry after witnessing fourteen harvests.

The young adults knew they needed liberation from the old bureaucrats. They felt disillusioned and did not know how to break the cycle. Mudi heard that Halima had offended the gods and was banished to Banza.

Banza was every woman's nightmare. It was the home of women who suffered from leaking bladders. These were women who had committed sacrilege against the gods. The custodians and elders said the women in Banza were being punished. The gods were shaming the women, the custodians often said.

Today, his cute sister was among society's outcasts. The urban nurses from the city visited Banza and offered hope in the form of surgery, but the elders refused the "strange" help offered by the nurses. No one wanted to help a person cursed by the gods or risk invoking a curse on themselves. Those nurses had found friends in Lami and a few others.

Mudi was moved to tears at the sight of his sister; he could not help it as tears rolled down his face. He ran toward his own blood. It was a sacrilege to associate with an inhabitant of Banza, but he did not care, throwing caution to the wind. If he would invoke a curse by hugging his own little sister, then so be it. Who cares about the rod of tradition, he thought. He whisked her off her feet and spun her around as he had always done before her marriage. He then set her on her feet and embraced her. As they hugged, his mind was blank, and he could say nothing.

Lami watched with compassion, Mudi torn between loyalty to the age-old customs in their entirety and his sense of injustice. These senseless beliefs produced people saddled with grief all their lives, she thought. Halima pulled away, looking around at the same time to ensure no one had seen them. She did not want her brother or Lami to be in trouble. It was a taboo to embrace an outcast, a banshee from Banza.

Halima turned to Lami.

"May Aminta comfort you in your time of pain."

There was a moment of silence. The only sounds were the moving river and the evening creatures beginning to stir. Each one of them was lost in thought, processing the events of the last couple of months. Today was the crowning event. Rolami's three-legged mob was winning. A momentary interlude, like an emotional scene in a stage play at the village square.

Mudi felt some warm liquid. Halima's bladder had given way again. She wanted to break away but he held her. She cried and whispered,

"I am sorry."

"It's alright," he said.

He was disgusted and angry, not at her but at the custodians, and at his father, a chief without sense. Destroying people's lives based on their false interpretations of tradition. Mudi had confronted his father over Halima's wedding and his father had said,

"Mudi, the gods are greater than we are. Our traditions pre- date us. I will not stand by and allow our tradition to be trampled upon by anyone. Anyone who challenges our culture will pay irrespective of who they are! I will crush you and any of my children who dare!"

Halima was distraught at the news of her wedding. She kept weeping and sobbing like she was mourning the death of a child. Mudi insisted that a hefty bride price should be paid by Chief Isti, Buzu's ally who was to become her husband. Buzu agreed just to keep the peace; he felt it was a reasonable compromise.

Lami got up slowly, joining in the embrace. They all wept, a triad joined by pain. After a while, they separated, collapsing on the sand at the riverside. Lami sat very carefully, wincing from the pain.

Mudi asked, "Why did you escape?" Halima stopped crying and turned to him.

"Which is more important, why or how? I don't know, but I now know I have offended no god. I am only a victim of ideas founded on folly."

Mudi said, "Why say this? You know if found, Lami and I will be in serious trouble. Go back."

She replied,

"Bad new travels fast. How could I hear such evil had befallen Lami and not come to console my friend?"

She reached out to hold Lami's hands, looking into her eyes. "Sister, you have to go back," said Mudi.

He was looking suspiciously around to make sure she had not been followed.

"Where to? Where to, Mudi? Banza? A place of pain and deceit founded on lies?" Halima's voice cracked with emotion.

"Don't say this, Halima," Mudi said, almost as if he were pleading. "We can't kick against the gods. I understand what you are going through…"

"…You don't understand, Mudi, but I do," said Lami.

"We both have found something you don't know. We are like two hearts beating at once. Today, you bear witness to my rape by tradition's falsehood. Halima has also suffered."

She turned her gaze to Halima.

"What have you seen, dear friend? Speak."

Mudi looked at Lami, flabbergasted as he looked around to ensure no one had seen them. Halima smiled at Lami who nodded her head in encouragement.

"Mutilating our genitals has not put an end to promiscuity. Rather it ignites in us an insatiable search for satisfaction as the horror between our legs only brings with it a feeling of numbness."

"It is not true," interjected Mudi, unsure of what to make of Halima's statement.

"Why do you speak?" Lami said, her tone dripping with sarcasm.

"You don't have a slit between your legs. Rather a pipe whose promiscuity can never be estimated."

"Believe me," Halima continued, "most of the young girls in Banza are promiscuous."

Mudi interrupted her, visibly exasperated. "Promiscuous? Who sleeps with them? The spirits? They are outcasts. Remember they smell and..."

"Stop that," Lami said. "Stop talking about them that way, you fool."

"Ignore him," said Halima.

"It is best for Mudi to see things for himself. Tonight, you must visit Banza. It is a different place when the moon resumes its duties. The same men who banished its inhabitants crawl into their beds seeking warmth and pleasure. A woman's body is hers and hers alone, what she chooses to do with it is not society's business. It's her choice. Can a woman be promiscuous by herself? Does it not take two? Why should one gender suffer and not the other?"

Lami gazed intently at Mudi.

"It is not true; it can't be true. Our forefathers can't be wrong," said Mudi.

He could see the point in their argument. He was beginning to doubt what he'd learned during his initiation into manhood. Listening to these women who meant so much to him made him start to have questions. He stared into space.

"I know how it feels when the truth one has believed their entire life turns out to be a lie," said Halima, slipping her fingers into his strong palms.

There was a long silence, as a jumble of thoughts ran through their minds. They all sat there for a long time without saying anything, deriving comfort from each other's company. After a while, Mudi stood up, his face grave.

"I will visit Banza at night to see for myself what you claim, dear sister. Heaven knows I will kill you myself if it turns out to be false! Let us go."

Halima stood up and embraced Lami even as she urinated again, unable to control herself. She tried to pull away from Lami in embarrassment. Lami held her close, whispering comfort into her ears.

Chapter 4

Family Meeting

Mudi assisted Lami on the long walk from the stream. As they got close to the village, he asked her to wait for him. He walked ahead of her toward his mother's hut. He approached two of his mother's maids and asked them to take her home. He also gave them herbs for Lami with instructions for their use.

She walked with a wide stepping gait, assisted by the two maids. She winced with pain with every step.

A few busybodies whispered among themselves as they recognized her and some hissed aloud with disgust. A few young women stopped what they were doing to acknowledge her. Some smiled sympathetically and gave her a hug with tears running down their cheeks.

Lami was well known in the village. Her ceremony had been postponed several times. She was vocal in her dislike of some of the customs, and that divided opinions. She had even successfully recruited many women who believed in her cause.

But at this moment, she was consumed with other thoughts. Her family was on her mind and the likely impact of today's event on them. Thoughts of her father permeated her mind. How would this affect his standing in the village? He was the custodian of the customs his own daughter was challenging. Would he disown her? What would he think of her now? How would he feel about her attempted suicide?

She shook her head to try to clear those thoughts. Every step was more difficult as she approached her father's compound. She wished the ground would split open and swallow her. She felt alone, ashamed and the dagger of guilt continually pierced her heart.

Usually, the ceremony was considered a joyful thing. All the women in your father's household would sing the songs of transition to womanhood. It was such a fun affair. It involved choreographed cultural dances, feasting and merrymaking. Today was different. It was so solemn it could pass for a funeral procession. She was not sure what her demeanour should be. She was not sure whether she should cry. Would those tears be acceptance of defeat? Her cause quashed?

She also wondered whether she should maintain a defiant appearance. Would this be viewed as a lack of remorse, leading to more punishment? Like most young women, her public image and acceptance was so important. Alas, she decided to maintain a straight face. In this circumstance, it was better no one could read her emotions. The faces she saw were all grim and gloomy. People shaking their heads in disgust, pity or anger. She decided the best thing was to keep a straight face. She suddenly heard someone screaming.

"How can you do this to your honourable father?"

"He does not deserve this stupidity and lack of tact. Are you a child?"

"What did you expect? Chicken brain, thoughtless fool, more worthless than my left hand, a child of shame!"

The voices came from everywhere. "Leave her alone," screamed another.

"She speaks for us all, she has borne our shame. I ask, why are women excluded from making decisions affecting women? Are we not their mothers' sisters and aunties?" a young woman said.

Gbosa!!! A dirty slap by the older lady, whose hands were lightning fast. The sound reverberated through the night, bringing everyone to a halt. The younger woman was stunned, falling backward from the impact of the slap.

"Shut your mouth, you child, and stop challenging the ancient traditions of our fathers. A woman has her place in the kitchen. Is she not lord and master there? Does the man ever saunter and prance like a king in her place of dominion? He knows his place..." The old lady said this with her hands raised, ready to deliver a follow-up slap.

"Slap me!"

The young girl dared, laughing aloud, moving away in one smooth motion to avoid any further assault by this old, menacing pugilist. She then took a defensive pose with her hands resting on her hips, rocking them from side to side. With her index finger, she pointed rudely at the older woman.

"Your place of dominion?"

The young lady paused to let the question sink in. She rubbed her cheeks, rolling her eyes to express her displeasure.

She smiled wryly at the old lady and clapped her hands derisively.

"Of course, the man sits where he likes in the kitchen. He tells you what to cook, as such jobs are too menial for his majesty. He takes the choice pieces of meat from your pot, leaving the remnants for yourself and the children. When he is done he leaves you with his royal mess for cleaning. You labour for hours cleaning and cooking. When you are done he beats you like an untamed animal who has never mastered his desires if you dare complain of tiredness when he is gripped by his carnal craving. Old lady, if this is royalty, I'd rather die a slave. Be warned. I respect your grey hair, otherwise, I'd never take a slap without returning the favour." She hissed, taking a bold step toward the older lady.

"Try it!" The old lady screamed expletives, moving closer to her provocatively.

The young lady walked away, seeing that things might become ugly.

The old woman hissed aloud and said,

"You want to die? Die you will, you and that Lami, a chicken that thinks she can fly will end up badly."

She spat on the floor to express her disgust. Some of the older women present nodded in assent, many of them hissing at the younger woman.

The maids assisting Lami tried to make her walk briskly. The pain was killing her, but she endured and walked as fast as she could. She didn't want to listen to these conversations.

Another younger woman opened her mouth to speak and she was quickly shut down by her aunty. The issue was dividing families. It was not Lami's intention but it was important that people talked about it. She felt some level of elation seeing that there were those who also believed in her cause.

"Lami! Lami!"

Some familiar voices whispered. She smiled at the sound of these voices. It belonged to her childhood friends Ritar and Lantar. She stopped to hug them amid tears. They took over from the maids. The tears flowed faster on seeing how their beautiful friend had been in so much pain. The abuse and curses were not making things any easier.

Lami hugged them tighter and whispered,

"I have always believed we were friends but now we are sisters."

They said nothing. She was shocked by their lack of response. Did they not hear her? Were they overwhelmed by grief and sorry for the shame that had befallen their friend? The sunshine of Rolami, the golden untouchable child. The one whose year of circumcision was moved four times. She had forced the chiefs to debate about the strange custom, but now she was subdued and vanquished. Each time it was moved, many nursed hope that their daughters would be spared. Hearing what happened to her today dashed those hopes. *Where to from here?* they thought.

Their only hope was gone with the whirlwind of the ancient past. One that brought stale, foul air and destruction in its wake. Will this ever stop? Every woman in these parts accepted that, although like the men, they were made by the gods to be inferior to the opposite gender. Women cursed and cried when they had many female children without any male ones. They considered women inferior even though all that differed was their sex organs. A woman who produced no male children was disdained. Female children had no rights to inheritance.

Lami spotted their hut from a distance. She saw her mother and sister waiting in the front veranda. Lami quibbled and her breathing changed, she felt dizzy and began to retch at the wayside. A woman ran out from a nearby hut and offered her water. She gratefully received the same and rinsed her mouth with it.

Her nervousness was palpable. She tried to read the emotion on her mother's face, but it was too dark to make it out.

She dismissed Ritar and Lantar, begging them that she needed to face her family alone. Filled with dread, she walked slowly toward her home, all sorts of thoughts going through her mind.

As she arrived at the front of the house, her sister, Lajara, dismissed the maids. Lami stood slightly bent over, looking at the ground. Her mother and sister stood on the veranda towering over her. These were the two women who mattered most in her life. They stood looking at her.

There was a loud silence. She could perceive they were hurt and angry. She walked hesitantly toward them. Her mother sobbed as she saw her wince with every step, Lajara watching with great disdain. She burst out laughing and said,

"You manage to turn a day of joy into a day of mourning, a day of pride into a day of unending shame—"

"Be quiet!" her sobbing mother, Hajaru, screamed. "Words spoken are like broken eggs. Once uttered we can't take it back. Lajara, you are hurt, and we are all hurt, but you can't speak to your sister in that way."

"I will speak to her the way I choose, Mother. For once, she needs to hear the truth, and she stands condemned before man and before the gods. She only cares about one thing and one thing alone and it is...wait for it, it's a surprise: Lami. Yes, Mother... you heard right...all she cares about is herself. The sun, the moon and the cosmological system must accommodate her whims and caprices or be damned. The beautiful flower unceremoniously plucked and trampled upon. Where was her guardian beast? Her immortal companion with the strength of an ox. The descendant of the three- legged animal. Even he could not comprehend your foolishness or save you from this odious calamity—"

Gbosa!!! Lajara was interrupted by a halting slap from their mother that stunned both sisters. Lajara instinctively rubbed her face with her palms, fire in her eyes, pouting her lips defiantly.

"How dare you be so callous? Yes, she is a brash, stupid, self-opinionated peacock. One who won't back down or give up but she is still my daughter and your sister! She thinks she's the messiah, the harbinger of great things to come. The one who brings the rain after years of drought. The one who ushers in the harvest. The one who liberates a dark race of fiends that cannot think or feed themselves but await the goddess."

Their mother paused to catch her breath. "Lami. I remember when she was born, it was a full moon. A shaman had earlier told me I was pregnant with a special child, only he did not tell me she would be special trouble. It's been from one trouble to the next. First, she would not breathe after birth. Then she started to breathe but would not stop crying and then she learned to speak and wouldn't shut up. She questioned everything. I hoped that one day she would stop and think; maybe when she married. She even found a young man who loves her. But she leads him on the slippery road, challenging norms we inherited from the beginning of time. A lost battle that will bring no good. Whether a curse or a blessing, she is still my daughter…"

Hajaru spoke with tears running down her cheeks.

She turned to Lajara who was still in a state of shock from the violent slap,

"… and your sister."

Lajara said quietly, "You slap me, Mother? On a day like this I still managed to earn a slap? Is it my fault that your crowning jewel has suffered ignominy that will be an indelible scar of shame? In this I understand your hatred and disgust for me, Mother. You slapped me yet Lami walks into this house unperturbed. You chastise me about spoken words being eggs? Even now I am like an outsider."

Lajara's eyes were bright with rage.

"It's me, isn't it? Blame me. The calabash is broken…It can't be perfect Lami! It must be Lajara, the short black devil. Who will get our father's attention? It can't be the unintelligent one, it has to be the brown and beautiful Lami? She gets to say the incantations during meals and gets the choicest part. She gets away with poking fun at the 'revered' males in this house. 'It's Lami' they say, 'leave her,' showing their thirty-two teeth…. But let Lajara try the same thing and hell will be let loose. I will be at the mercy of your caustic tongue."

There was so much tension in the air. Lajara was speaking so fast the words were simply rolling off her tongue. Lami approached Lajara and hugged her, which was not reciprocated.

"I am sorry," Lami whispered.

Lajara began to cry and held her sister. "I may forgive but I will never forget."

"I understand that you consider forgiving me is a consolation." She turned to her mother and said,

"Mama, you have said a lot, but I expected much worse. I am sorry and if there is more I need to hear, I will sit and listen even if it takes two harvests…"

"Enough of your sarcasm!" Lajara broke away from Lami's embrace and gazed at her mother.

"The superficial charm you used to con yourself out of trouble will not work this time. Tell your shaman that it failed to save you from the circumcision. Trust me, it will not save you from the rebuke and chastisement this day before the gods and man. What were you thinking? How did you think it was going to end?"

Lami looked down and whispered, "I am sorry."

Magda, her father, emerged from the inner chambers, his gait swift. The lantern burning in the room cast a long reflection of him on the floor. He was a lanky man with a large Adam's apple and a receding hairline. He had a well-groomed beard, which he stroked when anxious.

Lami saw him and her heart skipped a beat. She curtsied in the traditional way to acknowledge his presence. Lajara did the same. He asked in a loud deep voice,

"Can I speak to Lami alone?"

Hajaru and Lajara left reluctantly with their heads bowed. Lami's heart started racing. She began to sweat on her back and on her palms despite the cool breeze flowing through the hut. For the first time since arriving home, she remembered the pain between her legs and winced. She had been on her feet since she arrived at the family compound.

Her father looked at her and said,

"Look at me." His voice was grave. She had never heard him speak this way. She was terrified.

She avoided eye contact, but for the first time in years he placed his hands on her shoulders. He shook her with both hands and asked her to look at him. She winced in pain with tears running down her cheeks, and she looked into his eyes.

"Why have you embarrassed us? Why? Answer me..."

"I can't..." she whispered.

"The truth is heavy and it's a bitter pill to swallow, Father, I will not add insult to injury."

Her father stopped holding her and walked away, saying, "You must give me an answer now or else what they did is nothing compared to what I will do to you."

"Father, nothing can be worse... Father... Nothing." Lami was crying with a lump in her throat.

Magda said, looking at her poignantly, "I will disown you."

There was silence and only Lami could be heard wailing. She wished she was dead.

He asked again,

"Why have you brought this unbearable shame on our family?"

She whispered,

"It is you who is to blame, *Baba*."

He looked at her in horror and trembled, his feet almost giving way. He stayed stuck to the same spot. He spontaneously muttered,

"How dare you say that?"

"I do not mean to be rude, Baba..."

She paused, looking at him from the corners of her eyes. However, he beckoned her to speak up. His eyes were fixated on her.

"...I want to choose my words carefully..."

"—speak freely, Lami—" was his terse reply, as he pulled his beard fervently.

"...you gave me false hope..."

"...I gave you false hope... I see... Go on," he said, smiling wryly.

She looked him in the eye briefly, then took a deep breath and muttered,

"You made me think one day our society will put us in our proper place. Side by side with men and they will stop treating us as lesser beings when it best suits them..."

There was a brief silence and she sensed she was getting to him. She became slightly more spirited.

"Why did you not slap my mother around, Father? Why did you treat her with dignity and respect? Why did you not raise your voice? Why did you love her dearly? Why does she not have junior wives? Why haven't I walked into your room and witnessed you ravaging another damsel? Why have you behaved as if I were your heir, when truly a woman is worth nothing in these parts? Is she not just a mere commodity that could be sold and exchanged for favors or to pacify an enemy or a friend? Why did you not kill me at birth or pray harder to the foolish gods who gave a great man like you a female child? And what's more, a worthless, arrogant, stubborn one like me who was born years before her time? You gave me the forbidden fruit of knowledge and opened my eyes to the truths of our time. How dare you, Baba? How dare you! Educating a female was only going to end in misery. For how long did you think I would be quiet after I had suckled at the nectar of knowledge? For how long would I consider it a privilege to be wowed by knowledge? Did you not think I would use it to bring about change in my life and generation? You opened my eyes to the naked truth and since then I have clothed myself with dignity and class. What an error, Baba, I was born blind, subhuman, subservient to the gods' superhuman species called *"Man."* How dare I think I could dream of equality? How dare you make me aspire or envision glimpses of what a true society should be, one with equality? Where women could rule a kingdom, lead a home. Where women could also have more than one husband if they wish. It is your fault, Baba, and you need to change. Have I not overstepped my boundary by my words? Yet, you stand paralysed? Please slap my foolishness out of me. Whip me into order. How dare I speak to a man this way, how much more a man I call Baba, my father? Yet, he stands in awe? I should be beaten till I bleed out of all my orifices. I deserve punishment, Father, and you must do it! Whip the fear of the gods into me!"

Lami was speaking through the fog of pain, yet she persisted. "It's your fault, my father. You gave me hope. Why did you spend time educating me in the ways of old? Telling me about Aminata and her Amazons? Why give me false hope? I would have been married and had children or ended up in Banza; who knows?"

Tears streamed down Lami's eyes.

"Then I would not have suffered this humiliating circumcision…no…'mutilation.' I would have gone through with it earlier without force like the other girls. It would have been a distant memory. I would have been released to the freedom of promiscuity like the women in Banza. I would accept the complete subjugation of women without question or regret, simply because I would not have known better. You have imbued me with an innate desire to learn justice and truth. To bring about fairness for women like me anywhere they might be in the world. I cannot stop till we are liberated from the shackles of ignorance and traditions laid down by men in the name of gods. Had my eyes not been opened I would have been satisfied with a life of servitude and slavery disguised as norms. You would have had a perfect but broken daughter. Would you love it that way, Father? Would you have loved me more if I was in Banza or on a farm as a fifth, sixth, or tenth wife along with three or more junior wives? Or as a mistress to a big chief or three-legged animal promising marriage that would never eventuate?"

Magda said nothing. He stared at the shadows on the wall. "If it will please you," Lami continued,

"for I am completely broken, marry me off to a chief or an elder. But first help me unlearn all you have taught me because all it has brought us is shame and sorrow. Help me unlearn so that I fit in and not question foolishness. So, I can say like the market women in Rolami:

'All men are like that, you just have to endure.' Or *'this is our tradition,' 'it's just how it is.' 'It was like that for my mother, her mother and generations of women before, it will remain, Amin.'*

"Father, our world is not ready for equality; neither will it be for years to come. I wondered why I could not bring myself to be circumcised. I realized that it was not because I knew that circumcision did not stop promiscuity. No...not because I knew that a lot of women have high fever and die after the ceremony or during child birth. No...not because I knew other tribes who didn't do it and have neither more nor less promiscuous women. Or, have fewer deaths in childbirth, therefore, more children. The result is a much stronger and larger army and a strong agrarian economy. No...No, it was because I was denied foolishness by a father who saw no difference between a male child and a female child. Therein lies your fault, Father, while mine was listening to you."

Magda stood still. He had stopped stroking his beard. He could not believe what he was hearing: was this an awful nightmare? Was his hearing failing him or was he actually hearing these things she was saying? Was she possessed by a demon or was she now delirious because of the pain? He tried to speak but no words came out. It took all his willpower not to strike her across the face.

Have the gods punished her with madness? What gave her the audacity to speak like this? It may be the bitter truth. Because of her immaturity, she did not realise that it was better to be considered when speaking. It was better to not know the naked truth all the time. How else would one navigate life without the fantasy of lies and half-truths? What intrigue would be left? There would be nothing to conquer, no triumph over evil. He was transfixed in his thoughts, impressed by her answer but surprised by her boldness, especially in the face of the calamity she had brought upon herself and her family.

Hajaru charged into the room and slapped Lami. Lami staggered back and hit her head against the mud wall, shattering a wooden ornament. Her ears rang and she collapsed to the ground, wailing, her eyes wild with surprise. Her mother had never hit her that hard before. Hajaru panted; she was so furious and words tumbled from her mouth.

"How dare you, Lami? How dare you? Do you have no manners? Did you not imbibe any of the home training I gave you? What kind of child are you?! How dare you speak to my husband that way?"

She leaped forward to deliver another resounding slap but was held back by the firm hands of Magda.

Lami looked surprised and she began to wail.

"Do not hold her back, I deserve it, Father. You should join her. I have brought irredeemable shame to this home. I do not deserve your sympathy, I deserve your wrath. I am sorry." She sobbed, her eyes now bloodshot from crying. Lajara had never seen Lami this way, drained and without spirit, deep sorrow reflected in her demeanour. She was moved to tears by the scene unfolding before her; overwhelmed with grief, she fell to her knees next to Lami.

"You are as stubborn as a goat but you are Lami, and I love you. I forgive you," Lajara said.

Hajaru began to weep in her husband's arms and sobbed loudly. Magda bowed his head and held his wife close, comforting her as tears streamed down his face.

Chapter 5
Family Reunion

It was a frigid night, and there were few stars in the sky as Mudi walked the treacherous road to the hills. His trips to the hills were few and far between, so he should feel nostalgia but all he felt was anger. Mudi had always wondered: Why did fate or the gods curse him with such sour potion, making him the seed of a three-legged animal? How do the gods conjure such good from freaks of nature? From men who were only driven by carnal desires and who only cared for their bellies, deprived of all common sense by their rote desires. A society that never regenerates and eats its young alive was either in chaos or dies an unnatural death.

Why was I born here? he asked aloud as the cold breeze whistled past his ears carrying dust that peppered his eyes. He rubbed at it vigorously as he walked up the steep slope. He felt a firm tap on the shoulder and he turned around. It was a young black Amazon. She had large, beautiful brown eyes, and her glowing dark skin matched her plaited hair. Mudi smiled at her.

"By the gods, they have sent a goddess to placate me in my time of distress."

She smiled and said,

"You really look like the old man, the smile, the charm and I can see you are a connoisseur of good women like him."

Mudi's excitement dissipated quickly and turned into disdain and anger.

"Are you one of his many playthings? Are you one of those who give freely?"

He pranced toward her as he spoke and she stepped back, her eyes wild with fear. She continued backing away until a big tree halted her. They were both a few feet from each other, looking into each other's eyes: hers filled with fear, his anger. Her heart was racing. Mudi could perceive her charming scent, and her perky breasts brushing his chest.

"I am your cousin-sister, Mudi," she whispered. Mudi smiled wryly.

"Half the town is related to me if we begin to count. You seem to know me quite well; why on earth would you dare compare me to my father?"

"Our father, you mean?" she cut in briskly. "A man cannot deny his heritage, Mudi. You are a Buzu, and all Buzus are plagued by the demon of promiscuity. There is no shame in embracing who we are and our culture… Enjoy it. Nothing lasts forever."

"Remember the tale of the blind bat? Her offspring were not blind but she was? They saw life differently. The moral of that story is not to be defined by birth or heritage. I don't have to follow the ways of my father. Our fathers did not truly follow their forefathers entirely, did they? Many years ago, our people were all stark naked, but now we have evolved, and no one wants to walk around naked anymore. If the ways of our fathers are truly always right, why are you tying a wrapper? Why not be naked the way the gods made you and remain that way till you leave?"

He took a step back to give her some room to move. She edged away from his glaring face and laughed. She walked away, swaying her voluptuous hips. The beads decorating her hips bounced in symmetry. She paused, turning around to look at him squarely.

"Smsh!" She hissed and clapped her hands together. Resting them on her hips she said,

"Mudi, you only resist the inevitable. Can you dare deny the fire burning in your loins when you pressed against me a moment ago? I have been in that position so many times and I know a man who wants to unleash his urges on a worthy damsel. A caged beast with the facade of a sheep who for the first time smells raw meat and is salivating. Desire pouring through his loins, he holds back but for how long? Mudi, for how long? Buzu's blood runs in your veins, in our veins. All this political correctness crap is not your thing."

Mudi laughed. "Eeyah…I pity you, you are but a child. A domestic chicken pretending to be a wild fowl because she's plagued by the hormones of womanhood early. As our elders say, a chattering chicken builds no nest. Watch your tongue or you will be torn apart by wild beasts…"

He tensed his muscles, waving his index finger toward her in a disapproving manner. She laughed aloud again, resting her hands squarely on her hips.

"Would you beat me like our father would when he feels threatened? Yet, I am supposed to believe you are not like him? Your privileged girlfriend had her ceremony postponed for four seasons. I would proudly have mine next full moon and I will invite you. Brother, you condone Lami. You allow her to accuse our fathers of using women as sexual commodities. You let her call our most ancient traditions unhealthy and unspiritual. *Kai!* It is so insulting to women for her to think we are too helpless to think for ourselves. Or too dense to determine what we want or don't want, warranting social crusaders to tell to us what is right or wrong."

Mudi grabbed her wrist, grinding his teeth in anger.

"How old are you? How many harvests have you seen? You will proudly have circumcision next full moon? What for? *Eehen?* To stop promiscuity, they say. Yet you have had many lovers, you think mutilating your genitals will change this? Need I remind you in your own words you are a Buzu, and it's only natural to be promiscuous. Circumcision won't stop you, little cousin-sister. It will only scar you and perhaps make you an outcast in your own community. You may end up in Banza, as a freak of nature, a woman cursed by the gods."

He dropped her arms and walked away quickly. His mind went to Lami. He was torn. A part of him wanted to maintain the status quo, yet a part of him understood and supported Lami's arguments.

He whispered under his breath,

"These gods are truly selective and must be misogynists. They banish only accursed women to Banza, but what about accursed men?"

She took a few steps forward, following him, laughing out loud. She said,

"Do our elders not say this world is a theatre set up for the amusement of the gods? We all have our parts to play to keep them entertained. Boredom only leads them to mischief. Mischief to madness, where everything is in an eternal cataclysmic state of crisis. Are you a poor actor, Mudi? Are you boring the gods when you carry on as an unwilling hero who feels for the support cast? The extras? A demigod who fails to acknowledge his godlike privileges, but chooses to live as a man and to identify with the fickle mortals? I can't but laugh, and even though I am so young I know how fickle people are. In the market women's meeting, when Lami raised issues about this tradition, some egged her on. They danced, chanting her name as though a saviour had been born. Where were they when she was eventually hunted down and treated like a rat, cut and chopped like a stray animal with no owner? The 'great' Mudi with his fearsome temper could not stop the process. Are these the people you fight for? Enlightenment to them is a burden too great to carry, its ramifications they are not ready to live with. You do not understand the alternative, Mudi, but you are only driven by the hatred you have for your father..."

"And the love for my cousin-sisters..." said Mudi, his voice edged with sarcasm.

"What is your name?"

"Aisha,"

she said, rolling her eyes at him.

"Where is your father? The three-legged beast, I want to see him."

She smiled wryly. "Our father is in his harem; he hates being disturbed but who am I to stop his heir apparent?"

"Are you betrothed?"

"Yes, he wants to wait till I have undergone the ceremony and then we will consummate our marriage."

"How many harvests have you seen?" "Fourteen."

"How many wives does he have?"

"Don't know, don't care, fewer than your father has, anyway, if it's a consolation to you…cousin-brother, as I can see you finally care."

With a wry smile, she flung her plaited hair, giving him the "get away" look.

He smiled, shaking his head.

"Be careful, little one, and take care," he said gently.

He turned around to resume his journey, walking away slowly. He lifted his eyes up to the hills, looking at the house at the top. He suddenly began to perspire, a range of emotions running through him. There was a gentle breeze caressing his skin but he did not find it refreshing. That horrible vision started to flash in his mind's eye. He saw his father on top of his mother, pounding her because his food was cold. He thought he had gotten over this!

He shook his head in an attempt to try to suppress the memories. His breathing pattern changed, and he began to sweat, his heart pounding. Another image flashed: that of his younger self being flung into a wall by Buzu. This was because he'd held out his hand to prevent Buzu from beating his mother. His head had hit the wall and he fell unconscious.

Mudi's vision started to get blurry and he felt dizzy, as though his feet were going to give way. He saw his younger self enter into the house with his mother after a long day on the farm. He could see the young Mudi, ecstatic, tenderly caressing a glittering stone he had found. He could not wait to show it to his father. He pushed open the thatched door and froze: there was his father ravaging one of his mother's maids in bed. He screamed, his mother rushing toward him, concerned he had hurt himself. She dropped the calabash in her hands when she entered the room. Buzu got up and in a fit of rage slapped his mother and pushed Mudi out of his way with great force, smashing him into the mud wall. In anger, she returned the slap. Buzu, picked up a wooden pestle, smashing it across her face and then her ribs. He rained abuses on her. Finally, he said,

"From today, she is my wife, Mematha, the same as you. She is no longer your maid. There is nothing you can do about it."

Mematha was bruised and bleeding. She howled in pain and was no longer fighting back. Mudi picked up a small mortar for grinding pepper that had been lying on the floor. There was still pepper in the mortar. It looked like the tryst started while the maid was grinding pepper on the stool. He smashed the mortar on his father's head with all the energy his little arms could muster. Buzu turned away from his mother, shouting,

"You?!"

Buzu got up slowly as if in a trance, laughing hysterically. He staggered toward Mudi, some blood trickling down the side of his neck. Young Mudi spotted terror in Buzu's eyes. A part of him felt this was an opportunity to finish him off and put an end to the violence toward his mother. Mudi picked up a wooden spear. Seeing it, Buzu started to retreat. He flung it at Buzu, causing him to duck into the corner for cover. Young Mudi decided against any drastic action. He'd missed hitting him deliberately, then he walked away from his father and said coldly,

"Father, I swear one day I will kill you."

These flashbacks were so vivid Mudi felt those emotions all over again. The memories began to fade as Mudi could only hear his voice in the distance echoing repeatedly.

He was brought back into the present when he heard his name.

"Mudi!" It was one of Buzu's bodyguards, a stern-looking, tall, dark-skinned man. He had well-defined muscles and stood about six feet. He was surprised to see Mudi.

Mudi took a stance, poised as if he was ready for a fight. The bodyguard stepped backward. Mudi realised where he was and relaxed.

"Where is the old man?"

"At the rituals,"

the bodyguard replied.

"I would like to speak to him now."

"No one interrupts the rituals...I am sure you know that..." The bodyguard squeezed his face, anticipating trouble.

Mudi hissed and tried to force his way through. The ensuing squabble attracted Buzu's attention, who had been burning incense in the courtyard in the centre of four naked women. The women knelt down with their eyes closed. Buzu, realizing it was Mudi, said,

"Leave him alone."

Mudi, a bit ruffled, picked himself up and said, "I'd like to speak to you alone."

"Whatever you say in front of these men is safe," Buzu said. "They are sworn to secrecy. What do you want? The spirits are here and you are interrupting a fertility ritual. These women cannot leave empty-handed."

"The vulture only circles when it perceives the aroma of dead flesh. Do people still believe something good can come from you, Buzu?"

"You cannot address me by my first name, you cursed child." Buzu gritted his teeth in anger.

"You simplistic fool. It is the vulture's voracious appetite for the dead that prevents the spread of disease…"

"…'Baba' is not a name achieved by being a semen donor, but by respect. You have not been a father to me or to anyone for that matter." Mudi smiled. He was happy to see that Buzu felt insulted.

"I am not ready for mind games or a lesson in the philosophy of parenthood. What do you want?"

"The plight of your daughter, my sister, is a disgrace to our family," Mudi said.

"Is that why you are here?"

Buzu immediately turned around, and with a flippant wave of the hand, said,

"Speak to her husband, Isti. Remember, she is someone's wife now and he paid a hefty dowry for her at your insistence. She is no longer my problem."

"You sold your daughter to the highest bidder despite knowing she had a young man she loved? You are not absolved of blame for her current predicament." Mudi approached his father, but his guards stepped in to form a shield between them.

"Boy, you are difficult to please. You are like a sore that never heals. Like in one of those bedtime stories to scare children, you are like the crying witch who ate her child yet misses being a mother. If I had told Isti not to pay dowry, you would say I gave your sister out cheaply because I think she is worth nothing. I asked for a hefty dowry, so you say I have sold her. You behave like a scorned woman…go and talk to her husband, I have a ritual to complete."

"Buzu, my coming here should be a favour. Isti is your friend and trusted ally. If I speak to him, I swear by the gods there will be a funeral. You will lose a trusted confidant, so I suppose it's not in your best interest that I do the talking." Mudi smiled wryly.

"Funeral?"

"You seem to doubt me," Mudi said.

"I am aware of your tryst at five o'clock tomorrow evening at the edge of the forest plantation close to the southern border. I can have him ambushed and will have my men deliver his head to your doorstep after I have talked some sense into it. The problem is the conversation will only be one way."

"I have raised a son, not a murderer." Buzu looked at him, disgusted.

"You really think you are my father, Buzu? If it will please you to think you have raised me, then I will tell you, you have raised a man who disdains your legacy as an adulterer, a cheat and a wife beater. I would rather be called a bastard than be your son."

"You have been a bastard for many years, did you not know that? A son who calls his father by his first name is a bastard." Buzu laughed.

"You are the deputy chief of chiefs, does the plight of the women in Banza not bother you? Our women are banished because they cannot hold their bladders after childbirth. Do you not care?"

"I am never troubled by an act of god," said Buzu calmly and with a straight face.

He called out to one of his maids to tell the women to cover themselves and wait for him in the shed at the backyard.

"An act of god?" Mudi spat with disgust.

"Yes," Buzu retorted.

"Not all women have this problem after childbirth. If this was so we would have to raid neighbouring villages to get wives."

"It is obvious that most of the women suffering from this ailment are the circumcised girls married off at a young age," Mudi said, visibly exasperated. "The urban nurses who visit from time to time tell us that there may be a cure."

"Your naivety is alarming, Mudi. Banza is a place we established as a safe haven for women who society has deemed not fit to be among us."

"Do you know that some of your colleagues visit these 'outcasts' at night for sex? Your so-called gang of three-legged animals."

Buzu sneered. "I visit Banza myself, Mudi. Being an outcast does not mean they don't have sexual needs. And they are not smelling and reeking of urine at night, they are presentable."

Mudi shook his head.

"From outcast to prostitute? By the gods, truly, by the gods! Is this the god-sent solution to this problem, Buzu? The gods are indeed geniuses, perhaps even bordering on madness, I tell you."

"It's you who has gone mad, otherwise, how dare you speak evil of the gods?"

"Indeed, it's the gods that have installed Che-che as the governor of Banza," Mudi said.

"It's the gods that enjoy the commission he gets for leasing these girls to you and your colleagues at night? Spare the gods, Buzu, they are not that concerned. A man's destiny is determined by the work of his hands and a nation's destiny by having good leaders. We are led by fools, buffoons, hooligans…no wonder things are in disarray."

Mudi began walking away.

"Mudi, if the gods have no hand in our lives, if you had a choice, would you have wished me as your father? Of course, not! Let's not worry about things we can't change," said Buzu.

"Things will have to change whether the gods like it or not. I tell you, one thing I can change is the fate of my sister. Speak to your ally. Remember, dead men don't talk." Mudi walked into the night.

Buzu followed him with his gaze. He smiled wryly, muttering under his breath,

"Bastard."

Chapter 6

Gathering of the
Three-legged Animals

It was a cloudy day in Rolami. The first market day of the month was a day when the elders gathered to deliberate the issues plaguing the village. The air was heavy with expectation and tension. A dark presence hovered, and people sensed that something was about to happen.

The meeting of the elders was a very busy day for Kama, the head wife of the chief of chiefs. The first wife was usually referred to as the head wife. She had the responsibility of drawing up the roster to determine when each wife slept in the husband's room or prepared his meals. She was also responsible for maintaining peace in the compound. She settled quarrels among the wives or the children. Kama was responsible for the post–council meeting entertainment.

The residential compound of Goga, the chief of chiefs, was agog with activity from the first hint of daylight on such days. The girls in the compound had to ensure the whole place was spotless. As soon as they woke up in the morning they grabbed their brooms made from palm fronds. They spent most of the day sweeping and dusting. There was lots of cooking to do. Delicacies had to be prepared for all the elders attending the meeting.

Days before the meeting, Kama would commission the young men to go hunting for bush meat. She would smoke the bush meat to perfection and use it to make her signature dish: bush meat, pepper and herbs soup. She was renowned for this soup. Many of the women had, on different occasions, consulted her for her recipe. They also asked her to make the soup for them whenever they had any special entertaining to do.

The gods had smiled on the young men and there was lots of bush meat for this meeting. Kama decided to make an extra delicacy: bush meat and nuts soup, whose recipe had been handed down from her grandmother. Many teased her grandmother that this soup kept her grandfather at home. Her grandfather never married another woman after her grandmother, who was his third and last wife.

Some of the wives of the other elders had come to give Kama a hand with the cooking. There was so much activity and excitement. The women were chatting as they cooked. As the day wore on and the time for the meeting drew closer, the women served the spread in serving dishes. Some of the women went home.

The young children were very excited, too. They would hide in their mother's huts and peep at the elders as they strolled into Goga's compound for the meeting.

As the time of the meeting approached, the women put finishing touches to the meals. Kama went to inspect the meeting site to ensure it was neat and tidy. She rearranged the little stool with three legs, which bore the wine for libation. The stool was a special one and had been used to hold the libation drink in Rolami for generations. The stool was majestic and had the tell-tale signs of age. It was made from sturdy wood and its legs were carved like that of a big cat whose paws dug into the soil in the meeting hut.

One by one, the twenty-four elders arrived at Goga's compound. They were all dressed in their ceremonial white, which they wore only for the meetings.

Goga's deputy was the indefatigable Buzu, who had dirt on most chiefs and was in fact the "de facto leader."

Magda was part of the elders' council, serving as the secretary and record keeper. The meeting opened with the traditional libation.

The drink *burukutu* was tipped to the ground to salute the gods and the spirit of the departed. The gourd was then passed around with each elder taking a sip and raising the cup in salute. This was the traditional welcome. As soon as the last elder had taken a sip of the drink, Goga stood to his feet. He was about five feet six inches with a long bushy beard, with an arched back supported by a walking stick.

"I worship and pay homage to the gods. I pray that their spirits be with us during this time as we deliberate the future of Rolami. I salute our elders past and present. I salute our great ancestor, Aminta, as we pray for the return of the golden era she fashioned with her bronze sword."

The elders responded with a loud "Amin."

Goga turned to Magda. "Issues arising."

Magda stood up.

"The border: we have border infractions with Turan, leaving some of our men dead. There were reprisals by our young men on Turan's shepherds and flock who strayed into our maize plantation. This is rumoured to have been led by Mudi. The Emir of Turan is furious and reliable sources say he is preparing to go to war with us. He has sent emissaries to our mutual neighbour, Kampe, seeking support. It is unclear whether Kampe will remain neutral or team up with Turan. We are not ready for an all-out war due to some internal issues, which you are aware of. We are unlikely to raise a strong enough army at such short notice. It is also about time we found a more lasting solution."

Magda paused. Many of the elders nodded their heads in agreement with his comments.

Goga spoke with a hint of irritation.

"We will send emissaries to Turan. But are the young men not supposed to act on our orders? How dare they take such actions without permission?"

Danjah, one of the elders, spoke in a deep, croaky voice. "They will but we won't listen to them...."

Goga shook his head furiously.

"Danjah! Don't start the 'we won't listen to them' talk, children should listen to elders..."

"Times are changing, Goga, and it is important to hear their point of view and see where they are coming from. Perhaps an understanding of their views will be helpful. It may help us give more informed instructions, which they will listen to. In fact, we need a bit of youth and enthusiasm in this elders' council. We need innovation and energy," replied Danjah.

His words were not well received. Many of the other elders hissed in disgust, whispering disapprovingly among themselves. They complained about how they'd waited till they were old to attain the status of an elder. The young people must wait for their turn as well.

Magda, who had resumed his seat as the conversation was going on, got up and said,

"The youth of today are not as patient as we were. They want change now. It may be that they feel we have lost touch with the times. I hear that they are quite upset at the treatment of women—their mothers and sisters in our community. They feel women are treated like acquired farm implements that can be used and dumped like rubbish once we are tired of them. There is also the disgrace taking place in Banza. The excesses of some elders in this council with our tacit connivance. Oh, by the gods, do we forget that the golden era of Rolami was led by a female Amazon? No one in our history measures up to her, yet we have no female chiefs or even females in leadership positions? Perhaps anatomical differences are present between us, but I believe we are the same. We want to be loved, cared for and respected, and they want the same. In intellect, as varied as we are in wisdom, so are they, and are comparable if not better. The status quo can't continue? It is quite glaringly obvious to us all with plenty of examples. That girls given early in marriage have problems with holding back urine. They are then expelled to Banza because they have become social outcasts. Banza is a place visited by a number of us for pleasure. Those poor women are 'cursed' by day, but somehow the spell is undone when we fuck them at night? Banza, the land of prostitutes, is the harem of an easy lay. It is a shame that some of us want to keep it as a bank of easy women where we can unleash our unfettered fantasies. It's a disgrace what we men have done to this land. We have pushed and pushed young people to the wall and now they are on the brink of destruction. The threads of hate and violence have been woven into the fabric of their thinking. They consider it the only way to redress the wrongs meted out to them. We enjoy the best of women, wine and wealth and leave them with nothing. They are young, and we need to be careful as the fire in the bones of the youth need to be managed before it gets out of hand. I agree we need to come to the table with the youth and get them on board and on our side—"

"Enough of this proselytizing!" Isti interrupted. He was one of Buzu's allies and son-in-law.

He was a fat, stocky, potbellied man in his early fifties. He was not very tall so he seemed fatter than he actually was. He was always clean-shaven and well groomed. He wore flowing gowns and Arabian perfumes, which he bought from traveling tradesmen.

Isti prided himself as a stylish aristocrat. His family owned large expanses of land in Rolami, which he rented out to farmers for cutthroat sums of money. He was often referred to, behind his back, as a conniving snake with no scruples. He was Buzu's number one supporter. In his many years in the council he had never voted against Buzu. Buzu knew Isti as his ally to the core. Isti was often referred to in youthful circles as Buzu's muse.

Isti continued,

"You speak as if we have forgotten what it's like to be a young man filled with virility and energy, believing might is right. I must be rewarded today, I can't wait for the profit tomorrow. My gain is today or never. No sense of delayed gratification... It was only yesterday that we were all boys in this very village! Do you know anyone who is born old and wrinkled? Young men will always complain; what else will they do if they don't?"

Isti paused and looked around the faces of the elders. "Banza, the land of prostitutes? What nonsense, Magda."

Isti continued, "If I did not know you well enough, I could have sworn by the gods that you have drunk *burukutu* to excess this evening. Banza is a haven, a shelter for the weak, for those the gods do not wish well in their journey and who cannot live among us. Do not stand there and curse; how do we undo what has been done by forces we cannot see or hear or fully comprehend? We can only stand and wonder and be thankful we have escaped their wrath—"

"The gods have no hand in this!" Danjah screamed at the top of his voice.

"This is man-made! This is the greed and the stupidity of man who thinks he is better than all that the gods made. It is obvious even to the blind that we cannot give our girls very early in marriage. They are not ready for it, they end up in Banza. But of course, Banza is convenient for some as they can have a steady stream of women for their satisfaction."

Looking around the room, Danjah gazed disgustingly at the chiefs known to pay regular visits to Banza and said,

"How does it feel to be enamoured by people cursed by the gods? If indeed we feel they are cursed, why don't we exorcise them? These are our daughters. We discard them and treat them worse than we treat our donkeys. This is the trajectory of the life of a woman in Rolami. When she is born, she is taught from an early age that she is not a man and she is born for the service of a man. From an early age she is taught to be subservient, to cook, to clean, to never say no to the advances of her husband. Never to ask questions and be subject to beatings without complaint. The young men and women have questioned the practice of circumcision. They argue that circumcision has not reduced promiscuity. They point us directly to Banza in response to any attempt to argue otherwise."

Danjah stopped, then fixed his gaze on Isti.

"We all know the son of Daga who took the time to gather the number of our girls that have died after circumcision. He sought permission to come before the council to tell us what he found out. He told us that three in every ten women circumcised in our village die after the ceremony. What was our response? We told him we could not question the gods about the death of those women. We said those women died because they or members of their family displeased the gods. We, the elders, responded with brutal inhumane suppression. We meted out severe unthinkable punishment to all their youth leaders, so how do we expect them to listen to us? We men need to think deeply of what we have become. We are tyrants in our own homes and communities, ruthless and gutless bullies. We can't stand being told what to do by people who know better. Yet we speak of the golden era of Rolami fashioned by the bronze sword of Aminata. May the gods forgive us, but was she not a woman? Or did she have a penis? Did she not have large breasts that stayed perky even in her dying days? Isn't this the story we have all heard of Aminata? She led great warriors like Bajah, Mudia and Gorah to conquer all the lands around us and they all respected her. She had an infantry of female warriors called the 'death angels.' Their swift movement in battle could only be imagined. Our children sing about them every day. The likes of Ladidi, Lamita and Ranita who held off five hundred men in the battle of Turan with their bows and arrows while Bajah and Mudia sought reinforcement after their infantry were ambushed. We are sons, brothers, fathers, uncles to women, so why do we think we are better than them? Why do we think they can't decide for themselves what they want out of life? I am afraid of who we have become. A society that insults, kills, maims and subjugates its mothers is truly a cursed society…"

There was very loud murmuring among the elders, with some calling loudly for him to sit down. Buzu stood up, just as Isti screamed loudly at Danjah, "The deputy chief of chiefs is on his feet. Sit down, Danjah, we all know you have only two legs." Most of the chiefs burst out laughing.

Danjah continued speaking as if he were a town crier in a rowdy market.

Isti interrupted him, loudly saying,

"He that has three legs is on his feet. His gait is steady, his face is poised, and his tongue is sharp and ready to deliver the truth. Listen up…"

Buzu adjusted his wrapper, shrugged his shoulders proudly, and smiling wryly, announced,

"Why should I be afraid of who I am? I am a three-legged animal and I am proud."

He gesticulated toward Magda and Danjah who looked on in disgust.

All his cronies started another round of laughter, nodding their heads in approval.

"I have two powerful swift legs for movement and poise. When they see me bouncing, they know a god among men is approaching. The third leg, my oh my, when it arises and stands at attention, 'they' must bow and worship. The tripod is set, the trident of authority is complete. Until 'they' kiss the sceptre they shall have no peace. I am a three-legged animal and I am proud of it. I make no apologies, the gods made me dominant, the top of the food chain. Everything was created for my pleasure. The juiciest of all the game he made for my satisfaction is 'WOMAN.' I am a connoisseur of women, old, young, buxom, slim, tall and short. I have had it all and I make no apologies for being born great and dominant and with power, intellect and energy. When the gods made the domestic fowl did it argue? Did it not realize it was to end up in my soup every night? Yet, it plays around my compound even though it saw what happened to its father and its father's father, before it. I am a three-legged animal! And I am proud. No one, and I mean no one, shall steal my birthright. Like a lion in his pride I will roar, and all will tremble."

Some of the chiefs nodded vigorously in agreement.

"Just like the lion, mine is the choicest meat and prettiest lioness,"

Buzu continued. "I will be fair to all, but my authority will not be challenged. Women always need men that can handle them, physically and sexually. They need men to drive out folly and stupidity, to keep their 'well' properly oiled for the pointy end of the tripod. This ensures unforgettable pleasures. I acknowledge our mothers, but they need to know their place. Occasionally, the gods surprise us with an exceptional Amazon like our ancestor Aminata. A great female warrior who led us in the golden era of Rolami for thirty years. I acknowledge her. Sometimes the gods reorder the nature of things, but this is temporary, it is not meant to go on forever. It only happens when we as 'MEN' fail to exercise our dominance. The gods in their wisdom castrate us by giving us female leaders reversing the order of things."

He spat on the ground with a mixture of resolve and anger. "Over my dead body will the order be reversed in my time!"

Buzu swung his right arm over his head and snapped his middle finger and thumb together at the same time.

"I will not blame the gods and I will not question them, they are the gods. The women in Banza aren't the only ones given out early in marriage, so how come they suffer such fate? The gods are not fools! There are a few who are unfortunate. They are chosen to be food for the gods. There is nothing such people do that will bring much profit and their journey is destined to be hard. We are mere mortals and cannot change the design of the gods, we cannot do anything about it. Trying to do anything is an exercise in futility, kicking against a rock. We are the ones that get hurt. I ask you, my wise brothers, why did the gods not create us as bees? Has any one of you fancied being a bee rather than a MAN? Of course not, once a bee mates its fate is sealed, he loses his sceptre of authority after which it dies. Imagine being destined for only one night of pleasure and in the morning death awaits. I will make sure my night lasts for days. But the gods in their wisdom have made us men. We MUST enjoy the privilege and exercise the authority that comes with that position, Abi?"

At this point some of the elders who had been nodding in support and chuckling roared out in laughter. Magda and Danjah and a handful of the elders had stone-cold expressions. They were very unimpressed and disgusted at his buffoonery. Buzu, enjoying the attention, paused to allow the laughter to die down.

"I salute manhood, the gods are not mad. It may seem they have a perverted sense of humour. They carefully constructed our society for the survival of the best, to help cement our place in the sands of time. From time immemorial, men lead, women follow."

At this point, with a broad grin on his face, Buzu said,

"All the three-legged animals in this room rise in attention and let me see that familiar nod."

Still laughing, most of Buzu's allies got up and said,

"We are three-legged animals and we are proud." Some stamped their walking sticks in the ground for emphasis.

Buzu waited for everyone to settle down and then continued his speech.

"I charge you to let her know tonight, who is boss and 'sariki.'"

"In your case, it will be several women, Buzu, several..." Magda retorted dryly.

"I am not complaining; I am capable...have you heard them complain—have you? Is yours complaining?"

He winked at him and whispered conspiratorially, "Remember?" Then he burst out in laughter.

Buzu then paused, straightened up, and with a serious expression he faced Danjah and said,

"Let me be foolish for a minute and take Danjah and Magda seriously. In the days of Aminata, did she for once contemplate stopping circumcision? Is it on record that she tried to? Of course not, what nonsense are you both saying, what is all this noise with no sense…"

Buzu then turned to Magda.

"Is it not your daughter that has brought disgrace on our ancient tradition, Magda? After she tried to escape from her circumcision ceremony despite four years of postponement? Because of her connections in high places?"

Buzu let his words sink in for a moment. Then he turned to Goga.

"If we do not take action against her, the young people in this village will think we are unfair and weak. This will instigate an uprising."

"You must be out of your mind," Magda said, jumping to his feet and waving his forefinger at Buzu.

Goga stood up.

"Both of you sit down."

Reluctantly, Buzu sat down. Magda followed, albeit slowly, stroking his beard furiously.

Goga said,

"Let's stay on track and tell me about the well project."

Isti and a few chiefs got up.

Isti said,

"Chief of chiefs, forgive us but what Buzu has raised is important. A lot of people are concerned about Lami's insolence. Buzu has raised this issue even to his own personal hurt. We know Lami is a close friend of his son and any punishment given to her will also affect him indirectly. It is no secret they have a belligerent relationship. She has insulted our most ancient and sacred tradition and she must pay. It is important we show that any offender will be punished irrespective of status. Whether they are commoners or family members of the chiefs. If a commoner had done this, surely she would have been 'skinned' alive or married off immediately so she could be properly schooled by elders. As she is the daughter of the village scribe I will advocate that we do the latter. Marry her off to an elder who is strong and of mighty repute. This will serve as a deterrent to any other young girl who may be getting ideas into her head."

Magda charged toward Isti with unrestrained anger. He was ready to lash out but was held back by Danjah and several chiefs.

"You must be insane," Magda screamed, "if you do this…"

Danjah whispered to him,

"Take it easy, she is betrothed to Mudi. She loves him dearly, let them get married, remember they are two bean seeds in a pod."

Then Danjah turned to the elders.

"If I may, let me speak. It is true our daughter Lami has not acted in line with the traditions of our fathers. We understand her concerns given the recent deaths of several women after circumcision. Isti, in his wisdom, has chosen that a fitting punishment for our daughter is to be married off to one of the elders. We are all aware that Lami for many years has been unofficially betrothed to the son of Buzu, Mudi. Mudi is a rising star and a warrior, a leader of our young men, who one day will be initiated into this council. Let us allow their fathers to sanction this relationship and marriage. Let's make a big production out of it, a demonstration of commitment to reforms by our chief of chiefs, Goga. It will quiet the desperate noises we hear from our youths. It will give them hope that things are beginning to change in Rolami. If this pleases the court of chiefs, let's kill two birds with one stone—"

He was interrupted by Isti, who said,

"What am I hearing? Is Danjah suggesting we reward bad behaviour?"

He placed his hands behind his ears, pausing for a few seconds. "Soon every female will vanish during their time of circumcision."

Isti continued. "So, we may reward them with marriage to their young lover? This is not our way. Hardly is this a punishment. To me, it seems more like a reward. Lami will be married to an elder, preferably a chief, one who can control and tame her wild ways. Teach her to respect our ways and customs. Mudi is a rebel. Didn't Magda, in his report, tell us of his recent activities? Can we allow two rebels to unite with our blessing? That will definitely mark the beginning of the end of order in Rolami. Even the gods will never forgive us for allowing such a thing. I respect Danjah or I would have said he was conniving and aiding the young rebels. Lami needs a man with experience, one who has seen much of life and has a deep understanding of it. A man who has demonstrated that he has the skill to handle difficult women and control them." Isti paused.

"She needs a three-legged animal!"

"Over my dead body!" shouted Magda, his eyes burning with anger, struggling with his temper. Danjah was patting him on the back to calm him down.

Buzu did not make any comment, yet his face said it all. He was quite pleased with where the conversation was going.

Magda glared at Buzu, pleading with his eyes. He said, "Speak, Buzu. Why do you choose to remain silent now? The council is talking about your son's betrothed. I know you have had your problems with Mudi but he is your blood. Speak on his behalf! You know how much he loves Lami; do not let them marry her off to a chief with many wives. Do not let this council break their love and bond. You have watched them grow up since they were kids. Even the gods will not save Rolami from the madness that will take place. Buzu, please speak, we have our differences but we both must agree that Lami and Mudi are meant for each other."

Buzu said nothing, then suddenly everyone else fell silent. Their eyes were fixed on Buzu, awaiting his response. Buzu appeared deep in thought.

"All Magda and Danjah have said about Lami and Mudi is true,"

Buzu finally said, standing up. "It's no secret that Halima, my daughter, was married off to Isti to teach her a lesson. She was rude and insolent to this council. She began a revolt inciting young women to take part in the village wrestling games. She was betrothed to the young son of Goga, Bagda, at the time. The chief of chiefs did not object or lobby me to change my mind and I commend him. It is corruption to have a different law for commoners and children of chiefs. In fact, the standard ought to be higher for those in position of authority."

Magda looked at him with his mouth gaping and wondered if his hearing had failed him. He wondered whether Buzu saw this as an opportunity to reward his friend or to get back at his son. Stroking his beard, he looked around hoping someone would speak up and say Buzu had gone mad. He hoped this was a bad dream.

Everyone remained silent. There were some who would never say anything against Buzu, even if they felt otherwise. Buzu had a lot of dirt on many of the elders and had them wrapped around his finger. The silence was deafening.

After what seemed like eternity, Isti, with his rotund belly, spoke. "Can we have nominations?"

Magda sat down slowly, as if entranced. He could not believe what was unfolding before him. Images of Lami flashed before his eyes. How would she cope? He knew his daughter; she would rather take her own life than go through with this. He was about to lose a child. How would he break this news to her? Why did the gods preserve him only to see this? Why did he not die before this time?

Magda's thoughts were interrupted by Isti, who said,

"I will start the nominations. I nominate Buzu. I reckon it's important we keep her in the family given she was more or less betrothed to Mudi, and that may console Magda…"

Magda sprang up and rushed toward Isti, only to be held back by Danjah and several elders who helped pin him to the floor.

Isti was visibly shaken, his small nose breaking in sweat.

"It is a democratic process, Magda, and all elders have the right to be nominated,"

Isti muttered. "You, Magda, brought the laws of nomination into this council. Each elder, regardless of seniority, has equal opportunity. You can nominate someone else."

Danjah shook his head and whispered to Magda, "Do not worry, I will nominate myself. I will then hand her over to Mudi. The elders will never vote for Buzu. They may be fickle, but they are not mad. One hopes they know the consequences of this act."

Magda, who was trembling, nodded with approval. He sat down, asking the other elders to leave him alone and reassuring them that he would not lash out again.

"I nominate myself," Danjah said.

He paused for a few seconds, reflecting on what he was nominating himself for. He became gripped by a sudden sense of intense sorrow. Lami was like a daughter to him and he had watched her grow up. She called him Papa. Lantar, his daughter, was one of Lami's best friends. How on earth would he even explain this to Lantar? He had to do what needed to be done to save Lami in this situation.

"I can't believe it has come to this," Danjah muttered, his voice heavy with sorrow.

"But I am a good friend of the family. I believe I am better placed to teach Lami our ways and look after her."

Goga rose to his feet and asked,

"Are these all the nominations?" Magda got up.

"Goga, do not do this, I plead with you."

Tears welled up in Magda's eyes, deep sorrow streaked across his face.

Goga dismissed the plea with a wave of his hand.

"Magda, sit down, I have done nothing. It's the elders that have spoken. The council has decided, and no one is above the law. You have always advocated fairness and candour. You instituted the process of nominations and voting in this council. The chief of chiefs used to be able to have the final say, but not anymore. Do you want us to desecrate the sanctity of the council for the sake of your honour? We cannot depart from the process because it is not favourable to you. There are nominations in place. You have one vote, use it as you please. But in this instance, out of respect for you, I will abstain from the voting."

Goga turned to address the council.

"Is there anyone who would like to abstain from voting?" Buzu put his hands up.

Goga acknowledged him, saying,

"This matter is complex. In view of the issues at hand, I think we should allow Buzu to abstain. If you think otherwise, please raise your hands."

No one raised their hands. So, he continued, "If you decide in favour of Buzu, stand up."

Fifteen elders stood to their feet. Magda was so overwhelmed that he did not look up. He could tell the winner from the number of feet. He had lost all the respect he'd had for any of the members of the council. He was extremely disappointed.

When did Rolami come to this? He had vehemently opposed the marriage of Halima, Buzu's daughter, and lost. He had hoped such a thing would not happen again so soon, but he had been living in a bubble. This was history repeating itself, only this time it was too close to home. His daughter was the victim.

He heard the words of Goga echo, declaring Buzu the winner. He could no longer stay; he felt a tightening in his chest. He needed a breath of fresh air. What would he tell his daughter tonight when he got back home? Was this a nightmare he would wake up from?

Some of the elders congratulated Buzu, making jokes about his new bride. Some, out of respect for Magda did not make any comments. Goga, sensing the tension in the meeting, moved to have it adjourned.

Magda did not even engage in any of the usual salutations. He merely got up, turned to his friend Danjah, nodded and walked out of the meeting. He walked past the women who were bringing in steaming trays of pounded yellow maize with peanut and beef soup. It was the usual practice to have a meal at the end of every council meeting.

One of the elders who had voted for Danjah walked up to Magda, holding him across the shoulders to comfort him. Magda smiled weakly in appreciation. Danjah followed Magda closely, both with their heads bowed, their eyes deep and distant, mourning for their daughter.

The noise of the other council members placing their orders for the food and drinks filled the room. Most of them were in high spirits, their voices getting fainter as Magda and Danjah walked away into the night.

Chapter 7

Bad News Reaches the Nonconformist

It was a sad, long walk for Magda and Danjah. Both men were silent, each caught up in his own individual thoughts. They walked toward the southern border near the rain forest, where the vegetation seamlessly changed from grass to shrubbery to trees. They had both decided to take a longer route as they needed to come to terms with what had happened before heading home. Villagers going about their daily businesses who recognised them bowed, greeting them with the usual salutation. But Magda and Danjah were so caught up in the moment that they did not notice nor acknowledge them. Some of the villagers were puzzled as this was out of character for both men. They knew something serious must have happened at the council meeting.

Danjah slapped his face inadvertently to kill indolent mosquitoes, which seemingly mocked him by singing unwanted tunes in his ears. It was their time of the year, the blood-sucking insects unleashing their hunger upon the unsuspecting. It was particularly bad on days when there was a high tide. Today was one of those bad days and it felt like an army of mosquitoes had ambushed the poor citizens of Rolami.

Danjah kept his face like a flint, looking ahead and saying nothing. He kept on asking himself,

"What would I tell Lami? What will I tell her friend? How can I explain this to Mudi?"

Danjah's eyes scanned the shrubs, looking for the leaf used to keep mosquitoes at bay. It was like a natural insect repellent. Ironically, it was abundant in the dry season and scarce in the rainy months when there were even more mosquitoes. His mind was in a state of entropy, wondering what could placate his friend. He could not imagine that three-legged fool Buzu touching Lami. But she had broken the law. For all their posturing, it was only right that she faced punishment, but was this punishment fair?

Danjah broke the silence.

"Magda, speak to me and tell me what you are thinking, the gods may fill my lips with soothing words."

Magda began to cry.

"I can't bear to imagine him touching her, that unscrupulous animal."

Danjah held his arm and tapped him a few times on the shoulder. He frowned as he tried to imagine Buzu kissing Lami.

"Do not torture yourself with such dastardly thoughts. The more you think about it, the more helpless it will make you feel."

"I can't get it out of my mind, Danjah. The more I try, the more detailed it becomes. I pray to the gods that this is just a nightmare; perhaps I am in deep sleep. 'Wake up!' I scream within me, but the more I scream, the more my voice is drawn into this chasm of sorrow..."

"We can fight this. I am sure we can rally the young men for a revolt," Danjah said enthusiastically, as though it was a possibility.

"Revolt? Violence? But you know me better than this. I can't imagine sending the village into chaos over this matter. Regardless of how we look at it, Lami was in the wrong, she knew the consequences of her refusal and attempted escape. In her eyes, her day of circumcision was a day of sorrow. She calls it a day of shame. For most girls in Rolami, it was a day they wished the sun would not set. Many considered it a day when they were visited by a fairy goddess. There are many folk songs sung by the women which describe it as a magical day. Many women for generations have looked forward to this day. You have seen many full moons, my friend. You know the euphoria that goes with that day for most young girls. It is a rite of passage. At the crack of dawn and as the sun wakes up and rises, moving to take its place in the sky, you are considered a girl not entitled to wear beads around your hips or join the basket weavers' team. By evening, your status changes, you become a woman. Your parents consider giving you your own room, which you don't have to share with other girls."

Magda paused, his eyes gleaming.

"It is described as the day the spirit of our ancestors visits our women, empowering them with chastity and fertility. A day when the family of the girl being circumcised throws a large party to celebrate. How my daughter has managed to change this to a day of unending sorrow for her mother and myself, I don't understand. Did Lantar your daughter not concede to the circumcision squad? Does she not fight for young women's issues alongside Lami? It has in no way reduced her legitimacy as a fighter for the rights of women, has it? She has not made all the elders resent her and want to punish her, she—"

"Magda!" Danjah interrupted,

"Lami embodies the beauty and resilience of Rolami women. She carries the spirit of our great ancestors like Aminata. What is bestowed on her comes at a great price with disproportionate sacrifices. You remember the circumstances surrounding her birth and the events that followed? Have you forgotten what the oracle said about her at her birth? The likes of Lami are rare and only come once in a generation. History is silent about it but you know the sacrifices Aminata had to face. You also know the challenges she faced? Change never comes easy and the pioneers of change endure a lot. All the changes she advocated are not new. We have known for many years these truths, but could we speak up? You forget the hours we spent during various evenings of our youth discussing these issues, wishing things would change. Remember that every time at the festival of the masquerade we had only one wish. That wish was for change. We would wait anxiously as five harvests rolled by and another festival came up. We would make the same wish. Remember we had a discussion when we concluded that the gods had decided not to grant our wish? Did we dare share our thoughts with anyone? Did we dare allow anyone else to know this was what we used our special wish for at the festival? We did not take any action, did we? We expected a miracle or some magic. I feel very responsible for what has happened. We sat in the comfort of our homes while another generation bites the dust."

Danjah held Magda's hands, trying to drive the point home. "The status quo was convenient if you were living in the chief's quarters. If you were a man, why would you want change? You were born into a life of privilege, unshackled by theories invented by man for the gods, not troubled by the 'demon of the womb,' the insanity of menstruation, and the evil seductive spirit. As if men are not plagued by similar insanities. Is the birth of a girl a curse, a sentence of eternal subjugation to the dominant sex? We cannot deny the slight disappointment we felt as fathers when our daughters were born. Deep down we wished they were boys. It does not mean that we did not love them, we were only worried they would have to face so much injustice. We are not alone in experiencing these feelings. Many men are disappointed with the birth of their daughters for different reasons. It is not only because of what the girls will go through. It may also be because they feel that the birth of a girl does not improve their status in society or the extended family. It is common at wedding ceremonies for parents to pray the gods remove the curse of having only girls. We both know the horrible ordeal of women who have only female children. Lami stood for change when we turned a blind eye. She stood to be counted, though this may cost her life and freedom while we hid away in our homes and places of comfort, even though we realized that these were undeniable truths. We should have supported her and made her stand stronger. Things may have turned out differently. Maybe the message would have had a bigger voice rather than a lone one in the forest. Magda, my friend and brother, we must not blame her. She has done well. May the gods punish us severely if we criticise her for being bold, for being selfless enough to do what we should have done a long time ago."

Magda paused and shook his head as if not convinced.

"Lami is first a daughter, she is not a goddess, she is not infallible. Our description of her as a heroine is more fiction than fact. We love to create heroes, fascinating tales of individuals that act as a bridge between us and the gods. We see them as half god and half man. Lami has gotten this far because of you and me, her friends, Mudi and many others. She was never alone in this battle. We have put her on a pedestal that never existed, so no wonder her fall is so great. Societal change is a slow, gruelling process best obtained by guile and not confrontation—"

Sweeeeesh! An arrow whistled past them, sending them both ducking for cover behind the trees. They realised for the first time how deep into the bush they had travelled. They had lost track of time, so engrossed in their sorrow and conversation. They wondered if they were in Turan's territory. They were panting in mounting terror, gripped by fear. They looked at each other, wondering if this was their last day.

Who could have thought the best friends would die together Magda's mind wondered. He whispered to Danjah,

"If this be our last, thank you for being my friend. I could not have wished for a better friend."

Danjah squeezed his friend's palms and smiled rather fearfully. His heart was beating louder than his friend's words. He then put his forefinger to his lips, indicating for Magda to be quiet. They both turned their heads in the direction from which the arrow had come. Then they turned their heads in different directions, trying to take in their surroundings. They had both spent hours in the bush hunting for bush animals in their heyday. It was not the first time they would both be in such a dangerous situation in the bush. Magda pointed in the southwest direction, indicating that was the best way to go. Danjah signalled for them to wait for a few more minutes to be sure there were no further arrows nor an ambush.

Then they heard a familiar voice.

"For an elder, sirs, you duck better than the young warriors. They can probably learn a thing or two from your dodging skills. We should invite you to our next training session..."

The familiar voice chuckled loudly. Danjah hissed aloud, relieved it was someone they knew. "Is that you, Mudi, my son? You are a cursed child..."

"I was beginning to pass violent wind, thinking it was my last day on this earth," Magda said.

They all burst out laughing. Danjah and Magda breathed a huge sigh of relief. Mudi was with his right-hand man, Unde, a lanky, gangly, tall, dark-skinned man whose boyish looks belied his age. He was one of the desirable young men in Rolami. He had very long hands and his eyes were as sharp as those of an eagle, earning him the title of being the best archer in Rolami. He had won every archery competition in Rolami in recent times. He had even gone to the surrounding villages to take part in their archery competitions and won. He was admired by many of the young girls in Rolami.

Mudi turned to Magda.

"My father, I hope all is well with those at home and my beautiful one, Lami. I hope she's recovering."

Magda was crestfallen by this question, but he shrugged it off, not wanting to make him suspicious.

"All is well, my son, the gods be praised."

Mudi turned to Danjah and asked,

"How are you, my father, and my people in your home?"

"They are all well, my son, thank you."

"What brings you here, my fathers? You know it is dangerous to walk in these parts, especially at night," asked Mudi.

The chiefs looked at each other, not knowing what to say. "Speak, my fathers! I hope all is well. You elders say there is nothing coming from the skies that the ground cannot contain. There is nothing new under the sun, so what can be new in Rolami?"

They both remained silent with their faces grave. They were not men who told lies. Mudi was puzzled by their behaviour, so he asked them again, and again he received the same response.

Both of the elders were contemplating whether to tell Mudi the news or wait for him to hear it when he got back to the village. It would be no secret by then.

Magda was frantically stroking his beard. Unde asked,

"Who has died?"

"No one,"

they both replied, a bit miffed by his question.

Mudi, now rather pensive, said,

"You may have to excuse us as we are doing drills with the young village recruits. We would soon start hunting for the heads of Turan warriors."

He bowed to them in respect, excusing himself when suddenly he turned around and said,

"I remember that today is the council meeting and going by your attire, you are coming from there. You must have been disturbed by the events at the council meeting. I am not surprised. It is full of selfish old idiots, chief of whom is my father. Cheer up, your misery will soon be over when the younger men become eligible for council."

"The council has decided to punish Lami," announced Magda.

Mudi froze; he knew this was inevitable but did not expect it to be so soon and swift. He felt numb, a sudden tiredness from inside, and his legs trembled. He tried to hide his sudden trepidation, but his lips trembled.

"And what have they decided?"

He was met with a deafening silence. The only sound that could be heard was the nocturnal animals going about their business, as well as the murmurs of young men in the distance waiting impatiently for Mudi and Unde. The wild, nocturnal animal sounds seemed louder than usual; the croaking frogs and crickets' chirping made for an unusual uncoordinated symphony. The atmosphere was rather unsettling.

"I can't stand this silence. My fathers, please speak what was decided, hold nothing back,"

Mudi said, with anger and desperation in his voice.

"It has been decided, so it is no longer a secret. The whole town may already know the decision. The walls of the council are as porous as the baskets of the market women, please speak up, this silence is killing me."

Meanwhile, Unde was more eager to hear new gossip than anything else.

"She will be married off—"

"What?!" Unde cut in.

Mudi's heart skipped a beat. He tried to swallow but his lips and mouth were very dry. He felt numb, and there was a lump in his throat.

"Who was she given to?"

Unde asked impatiently, throwing his long dangling arms into the air. He so was overtaken by his desire to hear this new gossip that he did not pay much attention to the feelings of his friend. He did not notice Mudi almost losing his balance.

"Do not refer to my daughter like she is some wood or furniture to be chopped and sold to the highest bidder," Magda rebuked him sharply.

"Who is she betrothed to?"

Mudi asked coldly, trying to detach his voice from his tumultuous emotions.

Tears welled in Magda's eyes. This surprised Unde and Mudi, who looked at each other rather bewildered. He opened his mouth, but no words came out.

Unde asked, "Was it Goga?" Danjah shook his head.

"Isti?" Mudi asked desperately.

There was silence again, with the young men fearing the worst.

After a few moments, Magda collected himself and whispered, "No, it's your father."

"My father?" asked Unde. Danjah eyed him dryly and retorted, "He is not a chief or did he become one overnight?"

Mudi had slumped to the floor, shivering all over, finding it difficult to breathe. Unde rushed to his side, trying to sit him up, realizing the import of what he had just heard and asked Magda,

"Buzu?"

A nod from both men confirmed Unde's worst fear as he knelt down to console his friend. Magda walked over to Mudi and lifted his eyelid with his index finger and thumb. He whispered to Danjah to get the *mututu* leaf, which he crushed between his fingers and put into Mudi's mouth. The shivering and numbness stopped almost immediately.

Mudi looked up into Magda's eyes, which were filled with sorrow. Magda squeezed his palms reassuringly. The road ahead would be tough, but they were in it together. The moon shone brightly in the sky, it was a full moon but there was darkness among them, as they dreaded what was to come. They knew Rolami was soon to be plunged into eternal darkness and chaos.

Chapter 8

Not in My Name

Lami lay on her mat wincing in pain. She dreaded the thought of getting up and walking to the shed a few meters away to have a shower. She was febrile, with still so much pain between her legs days after the circumcision. Every step was wrought with indescribable pain. She felt sticky and irritable. She desperately needed a wash, but the pain she felt with every movement was incredible.

She used the herbs Mudi had given her but they only gave temporary relief for a few hours. This was worse than purgatory, she thought to herself. She felt drained and empty on the inside. She had hardly eaten in the last few days. She could barely keep anything down and she had no appetite. Sleep had also eluded her.

The daily wound dressing was the worst nightmare of her whole ordeal. Lankira, Rolami's nurse, used clean napkins soaked in salt water to massage the wound. Lami was held down by her mother and sister while this was done. She would scream and curse, convulsing in unimaginable pain. You could hear her screams a few mud huts away from theirs. After this, Lankira would then apply honey on the surface of the wound. She told Lami to keep taking the herbs given to her by Mudi as

"

they would help her relieve the pain. She also insisted Lami eat lots of guava.

"It will help you recover quickly," she would say.

Lankira was not really a nurse. Her late mother was known as "the healer" of Rolami. She knew every herb in the forest by name and knew what they could be used for. Whenever anyone fell ill in the village, they would send for her. She went with the midwives when a woman was in labour, particularly if it was a first- time mother.

Lankira had been trained by her mother. She attended to the young girls after their circumcision and nursed them to health. Of course, on many occasions as soon as she saw the wound she would remark, "Haditha must have been very cross today."

Some of those girls did not survive the circumcision. Lankira had a lot of respect for Lami, silently supporting Lami's cause. She hated female circumcision.

"Too many young, talented women are being lost to this tradition," she had told Lami's mother one hot afternoon in the market when Hajaru was complaining about Lami. Hajaru was shocked and became quiet immediately. Lankira was a woman of few words. Hajaru wondered how many other respected people in Rolami believed in Lami's cause. At times she had found herself wondering if Lami was a messenger of the gods as a redeemer of women. She didn't know whether to be happy for her "chosen" daughter or be sad at the sacrifices that come with being "chosen."

Hajaru's relationship with Lami had always been strange, a love-hate relationship if one could call it that. Since she was a little child, Lami had pushed her to the brink. She had always been opinionated, always arguing, always challenging anything she was told.

She had been referred to by her grandmother as a "free spirit." If you could get Lami to see your point of view, you had won over an angel. No devil on earth could make her change her mind. Hajaru had endured many sleepless nights worrying about Lami. Hajaru saw a little of herself in Lami and had a soft spot for her. Lami did get away with a lot of things most children would have received a hiding for in Rolami.

Lankira came daily to check on Lami. Hajaru found this a bit unusual. Normally, Lankira would show the mother of the circumcised girl how to clean the wound on the first day and that would be it. But in Lami's case, she chose to do the dressing herself daily. After dressing the wound, she would stay back and spend some time gossiping with Lami. This was an attempt to take her mind off the pain from the wound. Lami treasured these moments. They were the highlights of her day. Lankira also brought treats for Lami. Hajaru had commented that this was like rewarding bad behaviour, to which Lankira had responded,

"She has been through a lot. It's just to make the pain easier to endure."

Over the last few days, Lami had had nightmares every time she closed her eyes to sleep. The nightmares were about the hut of circumcision. She often had flashbacks of that horrible day. The worst part of it was that her mind kept playing back and echoing those menacing words of Haditha:

"It's a day you will never forget."

She would shake her head violently in an attempt to stop her mind from replaying Haditha's words. She thought to herself: *Is this miserable prophesy coming to pass?*

Was it really a prophesy? It was merely stating the obvious, of course, she could never forget the experience. It had changed her life forever. Tears welled up in her eyes often since the incident. Even the thought of going to pee would make her cry. She would not wish this pain on her worst enemy. It beat her imagination why the elders, especially the women, wanted to continue this tradition.

She had come to believe that the older women wanted it to continue because they were selfish. They wanted every woman to endure the pain they had suffered. As for the men, why would they want to relinquish their lordship?

She was now more determined than ever. Her emotions had been all over the place since the circumcision. When she was not sad and crying, she would become angry at no one in particular. Angry at the system, angry she did not end her life soon enough. Angry she had been subjected to this humiliation and pain.

She wished she had the means to destroy Haditha, her custodians and those old fools in the council. She would get worked up every time such thoughts crossed her mind. She would grind her teeth together and her breathing pattern would change. Rolami needed a revolution to shake it to its very foundations.

At other times she doubted herself. She wondered if she still had any supporters among the young women in Rolami. They would be scared, too afraid to associate with Lami and her cause for fear of repercussion. She could not blame them. How could she? Look at what had happened to her. See how disappointed her parents are.

Her father's residential compound had been like a graveyard since the circumcision. A visitor would think someone died by the sad faces and disposition of her parents and relatives. She knew that many women would be talking with their daughters behind closed doors, pointing to the shame that had befallen Lami and giving them stern warnings. She had resigned herself to fate, accepting what had happened to her. But she was now more determined than ever to fight this tyranny even if it cost her life. She could only pray the revolution would happen in her lifetime.

She had been home for the last few days. She was not looking forward to venturing out of the compound. She knew that she had been the subject of the village gossip all week. She had lost weight and her face had a few wrinkle lines in the corners of her eyes. She looked down at her breasts, then she cupped them in her hands. She thought to herself, they were substantially smaller than they had been a few days earlier. What a difference a few days can make. She looked down at herself, hissing pitifully, shaking her head. The little mound of fat on her lower waistline had disappeared.

Lami wondered how long it would take to recover from this nightmare. She sat up, supported by her hands, which were pressed against the floor. She winced at the shooting pain from that slight movement and the sharp pains from her groin.

She picked up the coral beads from the floor and playfully made shapes and figures with them. She smiled; the beads took her mind off all the events of the last few days. They stopped her thoughts from going wild. The beads were a welcome distraction, reminding her of Mudi who had given them to her as a totem of their love. When they were younger, they spent hours making all sorts of shapes and figures with beads and sticks. She wondered to herself why she had not seen Mudi for a few days. It was so unlike him not to pop in to see her or at least send her a message. She could not help but cry.

"Maybe he is angry with me," she said aloud.

She continued to sob, wiping her tears with the tip of her wrapper. She struggled between the tears to make the shapes.

I know Mudi, he must feel betrayed by my actions, she thought. She had tried to kill herself despite him meaning everything to her. He had told her he would elope with her. He was an integral part of the change she wanted in Rolami. A strong man filled with virtue, who had grown up protecting vulnerable women in his life from the terror of Buzu. He was a man who had learned to love by seeing the suffering and hatred fuelled by domestic violence.

He had told her to be patient, that he would protect her. She knew him, she knew he shared her views about change. She also knew that a part of him felt that they should respect the customs. He was not totally sold on stopping female circumcision. But he would not and could not tolerate domestic violence against women.

He had seen it firsthand with his mother and sisters. He had vowed to her that even if it took his life he would ensure domestic violence was stopped in Rolami.

Although Lami knew that no one knew exactly what had happened on the hill, she was filled with guilt. She dared not tell anyone. She longed to share the experience to unburden her mind, but she was not sure how it would be received. Everything stopped being a secret the moment it was shared. Her thoughts kept moving in different directions. Wondering why Mudi had not come to see her, she began to be plagued by strange thoughts.

She blurted out as if she was in a conversation with someone, "You are a coward. You are selfish. It's all self-preservation, isn't it?"

"Are you going mad?" asked Lajara, who walked in then. She had been observing Lami for some time without Lami knowing it. On hearing Lami speak, she clapped her hands, looking puzzled.

"Who are you talking to?"

Lajara looked around comically, as though there may be someone present that she may not have noticed.

Lami stared at her sister.

"No one. I was thinking aloud," Lami said, wiping the tears from her eyes.

"Are you crying again? I am surprised your eyes still have the capacity to produce tears,"

Lajara said with a wry smile on her face. "The tears they have made in the last few days is enough to fill a river."

"I don't see crying as a sign of weakness, it's just an expression of emotions," Lami said, looking at her sister, disgusted.

"I feel better when I cry, don't you?"

"Crying is not my thing. It's funny that people think you are this infallible Amazon. Aminta reincarnated. How I wish they were here to see you in this state, to see you produce rivers of tears in a few days. If only they were here when the nurse dresses your wounds. Hmm... They will see you howl like a wounded animal. You don't look anything like the all-conquering queen of Rolami," Lajara said.

"Lajara! Lajara! Lajara! You and your acidic tongue, producing caustic words sharper than spears," Lami hissed.

"The words that you have thrown at me in the last few days are unbelievable and unbecoming of you. It's almost like you have been waiting for an opportunity to insult me. Do you have to kick me while I am down? No wonder our people say when a giant slams you to the floor, even an ant walking past will tread upon you in disdain. You, of all people, Lajara! I warn you to be careful."

"I am now an ant? I see. Well, the giant that slammed you and cut you mercilessly has done a pretty good job. I am sure there will be a lot of time to reflect and cry your eyes out because the damage between your legs is gigantic." Lajara laughed.

Lami glared at her for a brief moment. She then looked straight ahead as tears trickled down her face.

"I was only joking, sister, and you know this? Don't you?" Lajara said, smiling.

Lami frowned. She looked away and sobbed quietly.

"You are a fighter, Lami, and I wanted to lift your spirits by provoking you," Lajara said.

"I don't want to see the crying Lami. I want to see the feisty one. The one that never gives up, that never stops even when she is down, the one who still manages to deliver the killer blow. That is the Lami I have known all my life, my one, true, feisty sister."

Shyly, Lajara looked down. "That is the Lami I love. I miss that Lami. I don't know this crying Lami and I don't want her to stick around any longer."

Lami smiled faintly.

"Are you sure you really want the old Lami? The one who in our last fight, got you bleeding after you attacked her without warning? I got you writhing in pain and got that mouth to shut up—"

"I was hoping for a rematch today," Lajara snapped. Lami smiled broadly, stretching out her arms.

"Help me up, I need to shower. I feel sticky! Where are the maids?"

"Making soup," Lajara said as she tried to help her get up. "You just plaited this hair and it looks all matted and tangled."

"I have been washing it with black soap," Lami hissed.

"You have lost weight, you look ugly, no curves, your boobs are now like slippers," Lajara said.

"Kai! What is this NOW? You are like Lami plus twenty years."

Lami winced from pain.

"Tell me about it. It's awful, there's nothing to grab and play with, no curves in the right places. Not very marketable. My bride price has gone down drastically. Baba will be unhappy."

Lajara playful tapped her on the bum as they usually played. But Lami instinctively hit her on the face because she felt sharp pain between her legs.

"You know how painful everything is for me in that area, yet you hit me on my buttocks."

"Just checking for vibrations, and making sure we will get some bride price. I reckon all hope is not lost," Lajara said.

"All I feel is a static lump of bone and flesh. We need to get some food into you before Mudi changes his mind. He must not see you like this. There are Rolami women who have backsides that roll like beats from a talking drum. For instance, Rakia's mum. Hmmm... now, that is what all Rolami women should aspire to have, a 'rich' behind!"

They both smiled as they sauntered along awkwardly. Lami was a few inches taller than Lajara and as she leaned on her it seemed her smaller frame would cave in at any time.

"Speaking of Mudi, I have not heard from him for some time now," Lami said, wincing with every step.

"Poor Mudi, he is still in shock. But he has been quite busy defending Rolami from the rogues across the border," Lajara reassured her.

They were almost at the bath hut when they heard Magda's voice frantically yelling Lami's name.

"What have you done now?" asked Lajara, exasperated.

"I cannot imagine it could be worse than anything that has happened lately," said Lami dryly.

Again, Lami's name echoed as Magda continued calling out. "He must be really angry. Has there been a revolt in your name?" asked Lajara jokingly, then to the general direction of Magda's voice, she replied, "We are in the courtyard, Father."

"Revolt? In my name? Why would you think of such a thing?" Lami was confused.

She had not expected Lajara to say something like that, especially because Lajara did not really accept what Lami stood for. She thought to herself that if Lajara could jokingly think up a revolt, it was not impossible. Her mind began to race again. *Who on earth could be leading a revolt in my name after all the shame?* Her mind immediately went to the one person she knew had the muscle and courage to organize such a thing.

Out of curiosity and to cover any emotions that may have surfaced on her face she hissed loudly,

"Who will dare take such an ignoble course?"

"A mad paramour...I think we both know who I am referring to."

"Mudi!" they both exclaimed at once, smiling sheepishly. They slowly walked away from the bath hut and turned toward their father's voice.

Magda briskly walked toward them. He was panting; his kaftan seemed ruffled, his hair was muddy, and his face had a few scratches. He seemed like he had been in a fight from which he emerged second best.

Lami and Lajara were both astounded. They had never seen him so flustered and they had no knowledge of him ever being in a physical altercation.

"Father, what happened?" asked Lami.

"Quick, quick, they want to wage war in your name. They want to foment trouble to avenge you. I tried to convince them, I have even tried to stop him, but he won't listen!"

"WHO?" the sisters asked in unison. "Mudi!"

"What stupid idea has he come up with? Has he gone mad?" asked Lajara.

"He is marching with his band of friends to Buzu's place and they are planning to set it on fire," Magda said.

"Why would he do that in Lami's name? His hatred for Buzu is no secret and that hatred is enough reason to burn him alive. But he has not done so till now, so why would he suddenly decide to burn his father's compound in the name of Lami?" The words frantically tumbled out of Lajara's mouth.

"Father, you are not telling the whole story. What is going on? Speak, do not put my life in danger. If the village realizes there is chaos and conflict to avenge my honour, you know they would rather get rid of me than allow Rolami to burn and rightfully so. Speak so that I can save and prevent people from losing their lives."

"The council of elders has decided to punish you," Magda muttered, averting her gaze.

Lami froze. She felt dizzy, leaning on Lajara for support. Lajara asked dispassionately,

"What is the punishment?"

Pulling on his beard, Magda's eyes sank further into his skull. He shrugged his shoulders. There was no good way of breaking this bad news. He should have found a way to tell Lami earlier. She may have been able to talk some sense into Mudi. But who knows? They were birds of a feather. He sadly muttered,

"You are to be Buzu's new bride."

Lami and Lajara froze. Did they hear that right? Lami became acutely aware of her heartbeat, and a shiver ran down her spine.

Lajara had known her sister would be punished, but she did not expect the punishment to be so soon or so horrific.

"But not Buzu. How can that be possible? Everyone knows about Lami and Mudi; it is no secret and they have the blessing of their parents. Has Buzu suddenly withdrawn his blessings? I knew he was shameless, but this is taking it to new heights."

"Buzu's bride?" Lami said. "Over my dead body."

Lami swung her arm over her head, tapping her fingers at the same time.

"It may well be if you do not stop Mudi and his gang of brothers from marching against the elders," Magda said.

"Why should I? They should burn," Lami said, seething in anger.

"They deserve every matchstick that will be struck as they are doused in kerosene. They are animals who eat the future of their children because of their obsession with the ancient past... Burn they must!"

She turned to Lajara. "Maybe this was the revolution that Rolami needed. It was finally on its way—"

"That is exactly what I expect from you, Lami," cut in Lajara, visibly upset.

"I am so tempted to drop you to the ground this moment. How selfish and inconsiderate. The village should burn for Lami? Young men in their prime should be cut short for Lami? Fathers, uncles, brothers, cousins should die because Lami cannot have her way?"

There was silence as they both reflected on the news they had just heard. They could hear faint chanting in the background. It was the songs of the young men. They were chanting war songs. The songs got louder as the men got closer to Magda's compound.

Lami and Lajara hobbled toward the entrance of their father's compound. They wanted to have a better view of the men as they passed or at least see what was going on. The chants became very loud and Lami was finally able to catch a glimpse of the marching men. The men looked quite fierce and menacing. They looked to the skies, marching in a seamless choreography without breaking rank. She recognised a few of the men and called out but they did not bat an eyelid or flinch for a second. They were young men of varying heights and shapes, but their eyes gleamed with sheer determination. Lajara and Magda held Lami up to help her catch a glimpse of Mudi.

"This must not be done in your name," Lajara told Lami. "These men have been bloodthirsty for some time now and have been waiting for the perfect trigger. This has been provided by the foolishness of the elder's council. Their decision is odious and devoid of wisdom, given your relationship with Mudi is no secret..."

Lajara, with tears running down her cheeks and trembling lips, continued,

"I fear this will not end well. The turn of events in the last few days may indicate the gods are angry with you, Lami, the bad luck is not ending..."

"The gods? Please do not drag them into this.... I do not fear my fate if it is instantaneous. I do fear being a coward and unable to stand up for my ideals or beliefs. How do I live with myself? I am not sure I was born for the mundane or to be married off and have children and then live out the rest of my days in a state of ineffectual nothingness, voiceless and tied to getting through the silly chores of motherhood—"

"Lami, you are not better than our mothers," Lajara interrupted, "and how dare you make the rigours of motherhood a mundane task too big for the likes of you!"

"I do not insult our mothers, my sister, but I do not desire to be one except when I can raise children who will navigate this world without prejudice, whom I shall teach that there's no difference between a boy and a girl and they do not have set roles in the society..."

"What about the difference between the fair-skinned Turan and the dark-skinned Gwoje?" continued Lajara, still crying.

"What about being short and tall, being of noble birth and being a commoner, being rich and being poor... Where does it end, Lami? We have to accept that we live in a prejudicial society and equality will always be a distant dream. Justice is a nirvana that we will always aspire to achieve but may never attain."

Lami looked at her, rather surprised.

"Why are you crying?"

"I have a bad feeling, sister," Lajara sobbed.

"I have this terrible feeling that I will lose you. I can't believe that I can't live with this realiation. Despite the fact that I still feel you are completely crazy. You are a stubborn, boorish girl who lacks manners. You do not realise how much you hurt the people that love you—"

"Look! There's Mudi," Magda interjected, pointing at the marching crowd.

Lami had never seen Mudi in a war outfit. He was a breathtaking sight, with those well-defined and chiselled abdominal muscles flexing with every movement. He was leading the crowd, raising his muscled arms as he chanted the war song. She could not explain how she felt. She felt shy, realising she did not look her best and had lost some weight. She did not want him to see her this way. She lowered her gaze as she felt his eyes on her.

Her mind quickly turned to the present. Something needed to be done. She wanted a revolution, but she did not think that this was the way to go about it. She knew the young men had been looking for an opportunity. She would not let herself be the excuse for such bloodletting. There was no dignity in being the cause or instrument for war. She felt a surge of strength go through her. With all the energy she could muster, she raised her voice and screamed,

"Mudi!"

Mudi did not respond and appeared not to have heard her. "Muddo! Muddo!" Lami screamed, now louder.

"Do you not hear me? Have I now become like this to you?

One to be ignored?"

Muddo was her pet name for him. She was the only one that called him by that name.

"Muddo!!! By the gods, do not do this in my name." Lami was screaming hysterically now. Mudi stopped in his tracks, turned to look at her and uttered under his breath, "Lami?"

He smiled wryly, shaking his head slowly. He looked at her like she did not know what she was saying, he then turned and looked straight ahead. Lami hobbled toward Mudi, with Lajara's support. He noticed from the corners of his eyes how much she was struggling, and his disposition softened. He left his crew of soldiers, signalling to them to pause and began walking toward her. When he was close to her he whispered,

"Lami, are you feeling well?"

She smiled faintly, a bit surprised. She did not expect Mudi to be concerned about her welfare on his way to war.

"Yes," she whispered.

"What is this I hear of? Mudi, do not do this in my name. Of what use is the shedding of blood and destruction of life for a lady in Rolami? A land where a woman's worth is equal to a few cobs of corn or less? This bloodshed is unwarranted. And perhaps the reason and justification for it should be made clear. It is well known in this land that if the council has made a decision, it can't be challenged or overturned. I deserve punishment, don't I? Did I not disobey? Did I not violate the rules of circumcision? I have no regrets for what I have done. I don't regret taking a stand for my beliefs. I am saddened that the consequence is that we cannot be together. But to lead your men in a fight and burn down your father's compound for the sake of a Rolami maiden is ignoble. History will not judge us fairly, my prince."

"History? You lecture me about history? History has never been about the truth, Lami," Mudi said, his voice cold as steel.

"It's a tale written by the victors of war so that their praise may be sung to high heavens by succeeding generations. It's an embellishment of facts, a bedtime tale used to indoctrinate a new generation with the culture of lies. I fear not how history remembers me. I do not give a damn. Today is the day I don't want to forget in a hurry. It's a day I want carved into the memory of all who live in Rolami for years to come. It's a day of atonement, and there will be blood—"

Lami, in a moment of sheer exasperation, screamed, "Not in my name, Mudi, not in my name! The elders have spoken and I agree with their decision—"

"You always think it's about you, Lami," Mudi cut in. "But the young men of Rolami have had enough… This march is to give them a voice… On this great day we will exorcise the demons of Rolami."

The marching men gave a rapturous applause.

"Do not worry, if you want the old man, he is yours," Mudi muttered bitterly.

"Is that so, Mudi? I did not realise that your love for me was so transient. That I could be passed on from son to father with such ease…Why not organise a threesome?"

Lami was visibly upset. Lajara and Magda were struggling to support Lami's weight.

Mudi threw his arms in the air.

"Women are complex creatures! A minute ago, 'don't fight for my honour, I don't want bloodshed' and now 'why won't you, is my honour not worth fighting for?' Only the gods have the capacity to understand women!"

"Mudi, how dare you? We are not generic beings that you classify unwittingly and make sweeping statements about, lumping us in the same mood state as a set of pots in the potter's shop for which you cannot spot the difference. I may be complex but not all women are, after all—"

"Enough of all this poetic lamentation," Mudi said.

"Your words are like the buzzing sounds of an indolent fly. I will not have you distract me from the goal, Lami. You of all people know how much you mean to me. They have forced our hands, and now I have no choice."

He turned towards the marching men. "Jorin!"

"Yes, Mudi."

"Escort Magda and his daughters back to their home. The battlefield is no place for an old man and two pretty damsels."

"Yes, Mudi," Jorin replied, signalling to two other foot soldiers to come with him.

"Condescending you are, Mudi. You know wars are won with ideas and not bows and arrows, especially one of this nature,"

Lami said, scoffing at him but knowing she had no choice but to turn back toward her father's compound. Lami stared sternly at Mudi, her eyes appearing fiery and all her wrinkle lines looking exaggerated. If looks could kill, Mudi would probably be decapitated. Lami was enveloped in a storm of emotions. She felt defeated, angry and disappointed. She was also very anxious. She did not know what would unfold in the next few hours in Rolami.

As they walked away, shadowed by Jorin and two foot soldiers, Magda said,

"Wars are won by arrows and ideas. Let's hope Mudi is willing to deploy both. We have done our best."

The sun was momentarily covered by a cloud as they made their way quietly into the compound, each retreating into their own huts with a huge weight of expectation in their hearts.

Chapter 9

Cryptic Deal

The day dragged on after the encounter with Mudi and his marching men. Lami looked up anxiously every time she heard footsteps coming toward her room. There was no news by bedtime. The only thing they knew was that Buzu's house had not burned down. As night fell, the anxiety in Magda's compound became palpable. The maids made dinner, but Magda had lost his appetite. Hajaru only had one serving, and Lami did not want any food, either. Her mother would not hear of Lami not having dinner. She forced her to have some goat's cheese and beef. After they all retired for the night, Lami lay on her mat but could not sleep. She found herself tossing and turning and having vivid dreams whenever she dozed off. Her wounds were more painful. She could not help thinking that the end was near. She had dressed up in her best clothes and had decided against putting on her sleeping clothes. She wanted to be presentable when they came for her, meeting her ancestors in her best attire.

She knew that with Mudi threatening war in her name, it was only a matter of time before the chief of chiefs sent for her with a white calabash, which symbolized death. The calabash contained poison. The recipient was expected to go to the sacred grove with the calabash and take the poison there. As soon as the person was dead, a cleansing ceremony followed to appease the gods. The bearers of the calabash get very excited sometimes. They injure or hurt anyone that puts up resistance.

Lajara and her mother had offered to spend the night with her in her hut, but she refused. She did not want her mother's last image of her to be one of her being led away with the death calabash. She also knew Lajara and could bet that Lajara would try to resist. She did not want to risk her sister being injured or mishandled by those stupid messengers.

Her thoughts went back to the events on the hill a few days ago. Why had death eluded her? Why was her attempt unsuccessful? Why had they discovered her? Had she been successful it would have been a different story. She would not be here, dreading a knock on her hut. She started to reflect on her life; as far as she was concerned, the end was near. It never boded well when the village warred over a female; she ended up becoming the sacrificial lamb.

"Have I lived a good life?" she asked aloud.

The last few days had been a living nightmare. In the end, she thought, liberty lost the battle to age-long traditions. She was just a fallen martyr, her distant dream of being a modern-day Aminta far from being achieved.

She watched the flames of the lantern in her room dance as the gentle midnight breeze came through the room. Her mind went back to her daydreams of being Mudi's wife. She had dreamed they would spend hours together in the evenings caressing each other. She would be his only wife, the love of his life. She had dreamed of being the mother of his children, living in a new Rolami. One that was not so harsh to women. Alas, all those daydreams would remain only a fantasy.

She wondered how things had spiralled downwards so fast. She wondered how she would cope being married to Mudi's father.

She hated him. He represented everything she was challenging and fighting against. Buzu touching her? She felt her body vibrate in disgust. She moved and tried to change position on the mat, to change her train of thoughts. She looked around the hut.

She had moved out of her mother's hut when she started having her period. Her father had given her this hut as a present. It was her palace, a place where she could be herself. It contained all her possessions. The beads she had received from Mudi and her father on different occasions. The wrappers she had purchased to celebrate the weddings of her friends. The special calabash given to her by her grandmother. It had been in the family from time immemorial. She was supposed to pass it on to her first daughter or her son's first daughter if she did not have any daughters. That was taken care of. She had told her best friend her heart's desire was for the calabash to be given to Lajara's daughter and not Lajara.

Her gaze fell on a trail of ants in the corner. She smiled. She playfully tried obstructing the path of a black ant as it walked past her. This brought back memories of her childhood. She remembered the first time she was asked to leave her father's side during a men's meeting. They had argued she was no longer a little child. She insisted on staying. She remembered how offended they became. They chastised her father for not putting her in her place in the kitchen.

She remembered how her mother came out of the inner chambers and yanked her out of the room. She gave her a good whipping and a stern warning to stay outside until the meeting was over. Lami had cried a little and then went to the back of the compound. She started playing with sand

and obstructing the path of several ants. She was there for a long time, what seemed like hours, yet the ants did not give up. They kept regrouping and marching with a tiny piece of sugar cane they had picked up.

She was impressed by this at such a young age that she told her father about it at dinnertime. He had told her to learn from the ants and never give up on her goals. It had stuck with her—she could remember his words vividly. Suddenly, she thought to herself, *Never give up. It is not time to give up. If I keep fighting, who knows, the spirit of Aminata may inspire others who may help turn things around. Even if I am another human offering to the gods. Fighting to liberate Rolami was worth the effort.*

She started to strategize and consider a plan. She could escape and leave Rolami, let tempers cool and continue to fight the battle from the outside. She would consider coming back at a more appropriate time. She was re-energized by the idea. Now she needed strength, as she could not travel in this state, or could she? If the gods preserved her till the morning, she would pay a visit to the nurse or send for her.

Her mind was more at peace with these thoughts. She smiled again. There was hope after all. She was brought back to reality by the knock on the thatch door. Lami's heart began to race, and she broke into a sweat. *Knock, knock, knock!* It was becoming louder.

"Who is it?"

"It's your father and I am with your mother and Lajara."

"Ah! Baba," she whispered.

Lami took a deep breath and replied,

"If the hour has come I would like to have *akamu* and *akara* first. At least I should be granted that courtesy since I am the daughter of a chief."

Her mother retorted quickly,

"The hour for what, Lami? Henan? *Abeg,* dress up, your father is coming in."

"He can come in. I am already dressed."

They all came in, beginning with her father, Magda, and lastly her sister, Lajara. Lami curtsied to her parents as a sign of respect. There was silence and it was obvious none had slept through the night, although dawn had not broken. Lami was beside herself with anxiety, wondering why they had come to her room at that hour. Looking at her mother, she said,

"You wanted to see me? It must be something urgent if it could not wait until morning."

Her mother looked away and turned toward her father. Her father said nothing and kept staring into space. There was another long period of silence. Lami looked at her mother again.

"Hide nothing from me, what has happened? Is Mudi dead?" They responded with silence.

"Am I to be executed or banished from Rolami?"

She was barely audible; it was a very quiet whisper. She was drained and tired and her voice was hoarse. Magda turned to look at her for the first time.

"I fear it's much worse."

"Worse?"

Lami asked in resignation.

"What on earth could be worse than what has already happened?"

Lami could feel her heart beating fast and her mouth was dry and there was a lump in her throat.

"Do they want us all executed?" Magda, acutely upset, said,

"They buried the hatchet…and made peace." Lami's eyes widened.

"That cannot be true!"

Her mother placed her arms around Lami's shoulders. "Unfortunately, Lami, it is true. Mudi has become a chief and he will be joining the elders' council at the expense of…your father."

Lami was shocked to hear this. She felt her feet swaying and she was finding it difficult to maintain her balance. Tired, she slumped to the floor and felt instant pain from her injury. She yelled and began to sob. She felt like wailing aloud but she knew it was unfair to wake the neighbours. Her mother squeezed her shoulders to comfort her.

"Kai! It can't be true. Father, I am so sorry. We must challenge this. It is not my father's fault! Why should he be punished because of me? It is unjust, draconian…"

"The decision of the council stands," said her mother matter-of-factly.

"There was no fight, no war, and no bloodshed," Magda said.

"Mudi and Buzu had no fights, no swords clashed. The only sounds heard were the clattering of calabashes filled with palm wine. And a truce was brokered and the council was called to an emergency meeting. Mudi was elevated and your father deposed. They agreed to allow the urban nurses come into Banza to help the women. The medical solution proposed by the nurses must be presented to the council for approval first. They also allowed formal engagements between ten of Mudi's men and their girlfriends."

"Mudi is no scribe," Lami said, weeping.

"He can't even remember what he had for lunch the day before. He's barely literate. I taught him everything he knows; these were all my ideas. I called it a fallback plan, it was my plan C. Mudi steals my ideas without acknowledging me."

"Isti is the new scribe," added Magda. "He betrayed me,"

Lami continued, as though she did not hear her father.

"He sold me out to make himself a hero and now I am damned. I am to spend the rest of my life in purgatory being one of the many sex slaves in the house of the three-legged animal Buzu, his father…"

"It's not as bad as we had thought it would be," Lajara said. "At least you are alive—"

Lami jerked away angrily from her mother's embrace.

"How dare you, Lajara? How dare you? I see your wishes have come true. Now that I am 'dead' you could not even wait for my body to go cold before you began spitting on my corpse? You jealous little brat! You will always be in my shadows. What I have achieved in this life I give you three lifetimes and you will not have accomplished half. Oh! You can't wait to gloat. Many women in Rolami can't wait to laugh. Their laughter will be heard in Turan and our neighbours will think we have gone mad. With the likes of you, who needs enemies? Please leave me alone, all of you."

"You have misconstrued what I said," Lajara said, deep sadness in her voice.

"I am only happy and relieved that you are alive, my sister, that's all. I hate your guts and we have had our differences over the years. But I wouldn't even wish my enemy a lifetime with the so called three-legged animal. A man who is sex-crazed and believes the most basic drive is the most critical thing in life. A fool who believes all women must respond to a show of sexual strength."

Lajara recoiled in disgust at these words. Even for her, Buzu represented evil. She clapped her hands three times in front of her as a sign of disgust.

"A three-legged fool for a brother-in-law? Kai! The gods forbid! He and his compatriots are men driven only by their carnal desire. Men who objectify women and see them as sex objects and for servitude. They are cowards who are scared to see the order change. They know deep down that change means women will stand side by side with them in all coveted places in society. They cannot stomach such a change, they fear the loss of their privilege. But I do believe a woman's role as mother and homemaker is a great role. But a man can be a cook, be a great father and a homemaker, too. Why not? You do not need two heads to fulfill these roles nor do you need a vagina."

"You speak with the two corners of your mouth, little sister!

You speak as if you truly want equality,"

Lami angrily retorted. "Do you really know what it means for a man and woman to stand side by side without prejudice? To be judged without preconceived stereotypes about your ability and looks? No, you don't know, my sister. Please, can you all leave me alone? I need my space."

There was a brief silence as they all gazed at each other, then Lami looked away angrily, fire burning in her eyes.

"You are an arrogant bitch," Magda said.

Everyone was aghast, including Lami. Magda never used strong words, he hardly ever spoke harshly to anyone, especially Lami.

Lami was immediately on her knees before Magda. "Father, what have I done to deserve these strong words?"

"Be quiet! I have listened to your rant for a long time and I will not be a father if I do not tell you the truth. You think you are some hero or martyr. But you are just a self-absolved little girl who likes to hear the sound of her voice," Magda said.

"Equality, equality, you and your cronies scream from the rooftops, crying foul at every action or inaction. Change comes by the power of silent graceful persistence. Look at Riskatta, Jatau's widow. The tradition was for her brothers-in-law to inherit his property. She continued to appeal to the council till they granted her request. That victory opened the door for women to inherit their husband's assets. Do you know how many elders she courted? Do you know how many deals were done behind closed doors to bring it to pass? Now, no Rolami woman needs to bed elders to receive their inheritance. This, Lami, is how to get the 'equality' you crave. It is not by making trouble without sense and putting us through hell. Have you ever considered what I would have gone through over the years in those council meetings? All because of your stance? Have you ever said thank you to us for the support? Do you realise what I have endured, rather, what we all have endured? By the gods, we wake up asking ourselves what would become of you. I have lived in fear for years hoping one day this would not happen. Do you understand what your mother and I have endured for your sake? Do we ever complain?"

Tears streamed down Lami's face, forming a puddle on the floor. Her mother sank to the ground beside her and drew her into an embrace, placing Lami's head on her chest. She looked up at her husband and said very softly, "Magda, Magda my love, that is enough". She sounded almost like she was wooing him. She reached out and held his hands, squeezing it gently.

She looked from one daughter to the other.

"You are hurt, my daughters, but words are like eggs, once they fall to the ground and crack, they cannot be taken back. I have always told you to consider your words carefully before you speak. We should not reverse the order of things; a man is a man. It's how the gods have ordered things, and we gain nothing from challenging the gods." She turned to her husband.

"Magda, I think it is time we told them. It will be no secret by daybreak and it's better they hear it from us."

He immediately understood what she was talking about; he sighed and nodded in agreement.

"Lami and Lajara, listen to me carefully, you know how much we love you. We have kept this from you to protect you both. But the hour has come for us to reveal this truth because it may soon be said from the rooftops. Some bad people may begin to refer to my origin to create mischief." She paused.

There was silence.

Lami and Lajara had their gazes fixed on their mother. After a moment,

Lami asked,

"That you are half-Turan?" Hajaru was visibly surprised. Lami said,

"We have always known, Mum. The rumor mill never stops in Rolami. The gossip is nonstop at the village square, the markets, at the streams and riverbanks. Even if you are deaf, you certainly will perceive the whispers. It was pretty obvious considering that most of your relatives are across the border."

"How long have you known?"

Hajaru asked, still perplexed that her daughters knew, despite her persistent denial whenever they quizzed her as younger kids. She'd even gone as far as swearing on her father's grave.

"Mama, you don't look like a typical Rolami woman, your skin complexion, facial features, your funny accent..."

Mentioning her accent, Hajaru raised her hand as if wanting to give Lajara a playful slap.

Lami continued, "More importantly, it's is well documented that Turan women are not circumcised—"

"Let me finish, Lami—"

"Does that mean you are not circumcised?" Lajara asked angrily.

"No, I am not circumcised and I am not promiscuous... so circumcision and promiscuity are not linked."

Lami instinctively moved away from her mother, wincing in pain as she did so. She covered her face with both her palms as she spoke between her teeth. "You betrayed me. Mother, you lied to me, and you knew all along that this was a farce, but you kept on saying hurtful things about my crusade to free the women of Rolami. You knew the truth... Why did you not at least assure me that I was on the right path? Why were you my most vocal critique in this house and even in public? Little wonder the nurse always looked at you funny! You saw no reason why I should not be circumcised like all the other girls. You told me to stop being stubborn and obey the custom, Haba! Mother, Mother, why?"

Hajaru was already shedding tears.

"I did not have a choice. Your father's position as scribe was in jeopardy the moment Buzu knew I was not circumcised..."

The girls both looked up at their mother, stunned.

"How would he have known? Do not tell me you patronised that bastard in search for a male child?"

Interjected Lajara, a hint of disappointment in her voice.

"Mematha told him. It was a long time ago during a heated argument about circumcision and promiscuity. He did beat her to a pulp and then confronted Magda. He threatened to tell everyone who cared to listen, and he would have lost his position as the scribe. You know your father cannot tell a lie, so he did not deny that it was true. He pleaded with Buzu not to disclose this to anyone in exchange for support of Buzu in council meetings. Buzu became influential in the council with many of his ideologies unchallenged. Over the years, dying chiefs were replaced with his cronies. A few years ago, when Lami started to challenge the status quo, Buzu came to Magda, accusing him of using you as a proxy to fight him and threatened to make me undergo circumcision at my age, but alas he has replaced your father with his son."

Hajaru collapsed on the floor in tears. Lajara knelt as well and they all cried.

Magda leaned against the wall, looking at the three women in his life. He then turned to look into the distance at nothing in particular. There was an uneasy calm in his posture and his face was expressionless.

Chapter 10

Stages of Grief

The room was dark with no light filtering through. The window had been blocked out with dry thatch at Lami's request. It was eerily quiet, the air was stale, and it had become the room of sorrow. Lami sat, coiled up in a corner, and her face was pale and her eyes sunken. Her plaited hair was unkempt, and she drank water sparingly. She was a shadow of herself. She had become quite emaciated, rarely leaving the room except to have a shower and sometimes when her father insisted she have dinner with the family. She had not left the compound since her circumcision a few weeks ago. She had turned herself into a recluse.

She was becoming weak, erratic and unpredictable. She was deeply hurt by the betrayal of Mudi and in some ways her parents. Unable to find the courage to face the outside world, its gossip and criticism, she was also terrified about being a junior wife in Buzu's house. She remembered the experience of Halima, who was beaten every day by the more senior wives. How could she become a junior wife to aunty Mematha? She was like her mother.

The worst fear was that she could not imagine Buzu touching her; she cringed at the very thought of it. Oh, how

Buzu would make fun of her constantly. He would feel like a conqueror. He would ensure her life was miserable. She often thought to herself whether death was not better than this. She also reflected on her plan to leave Rolami. She had healed well, and the plan became more attractive as the days went by.

Her heart had been eaten by sadness. Mudi, the love of her life, had betrayed her. Each day when the maids came to clean her room she asked about Mudi. They had little news. She wondered whether they were telling her the truth. She had become quite anxious. She would walk toward the door whenever she heard footsteps, hoping it was Mudi. She had also sent mutual friends to him to allow her audience, but instead he snubbed her. She pressed Lajara for information about Mudi. At first, Lajara said nothing, but Lami saw through her and she had no choice but to tell her what she had heard.

There were rumours around town that Mudi was "sowing his wild oats in Banza." This was so out of character for Mudi, whose escapades even surprised Buzu. Buzu remarked to his friend Isti,

"Alas, Mudi is not a bastard but the true son of his father."

Buzu was finally pleased that Mudi had seen reason, and that made him proud. He'd often said that Lami was a bad influence on Mudi, making him fall out of favour with the gods.

"Just a little while, I will put Lami on the right track."

Rolami was abuzz with talk about Mudi's escapades, but Lami refused to believe even when she was told by Lajara. She continued to live in denial.

"These are just rumours designed to taint Mudi's name."

This went on for a while, until Lajara gave up and steered any conversations she had with Lami away from the subject of Mudi.

For the last few days, Lami's mind had been focused on escaping from Rolami. This would at least guarantee she did not marry Buzu. She went to her mother's hut one evening to her mother's surprise and started to ask Hajaru questions about her relatives. Hajaru was puzzled by the sudden interest in her family but did not think much of it. She was only too happy that Lami was being a bit more social.

This warm morning, Lami had taken her morning shower. She was settling into her usual solitary routine, with her thoughts being her only companion. Lajara came to her door and announced that she had an important visitor.

"Go away," Lami screamed, adding that Lajara, of all people, knew she did not want to see anyone. Lajara forced the door open, allowing light into the room. Lami was temporarily blinded by the light as she had been in the dark for a while. She lunged toward the door to shut out the light.

"Lami?"

She paused. "Halima?"

She hurried toward the direction of the voice. Lajara stepped out of the way quickly. They were locked in embrace for a few seconds. Halima pulled away and held Lami at arm's length, looking at her face.

"Lami! Oh, Lami! How I have missed you!"

She pulled her into another embrace. They held each other for a while. Lami was so happy to see her friend after such a long time. She had not smiled in a long while and she found it so wonderful to smile.

"By the gods, this cannot be you, you are a shadow of yourself, girl. Lami, what happened to you?"

She scrunched up her nose in the funny way she did when they were younger.

"You look awful. Living in the dark? What is this, Lami? What has happened to my sunshine?"

Halima moved to the window and removed the covering, letting in the rays of the sun. Lami squinted as she looked toward the windows. It was a beautiful morning. She had been trapped in this room for so long that she had ceased to appreciate nature. Halima walked around the room, moving one item here and there to try to make it look more presentable.

Halima wore a beautiful brown wrapper, which clung tightly to her rounded hips. Her black hair was beautifully plaited and filled with color-coordinated beads. She had beads around her long dark neck and on her hips. Her flat, cute nose bore a large ring, and her arms and forearms had healing scarification marks.

Lami was so pleased to see Halima, who looked much better than the last time she saw her by the stream. Lami looked at herself and for the first time noticed how shabby she looked now. She instinctively adjusted her braids with her hands to make them look a little neater. Smiling, she said,

"And you, you look much better, revived, the sun has risen in the house of the Buzus."

Lami said this with a wry smile.

"Do not say such a thing,"

Halima said. "It's a thing of shame. I cannot imagine all that has happened in the last few weeks. I would not have thought Mudi was a scheming bastard. I hate him for what he did to you."

"Did he really have a choice? It would have led to needless bloodshed—"

"Buzu has no shame!"

Halima hissed.

"Buzu did not spare you or your mother shame and ridicule. He hates me with a passion. Will he not at the slightest opportunity give the same to Mudi and me in unbridled amounts? Given how difficult we were making things for his council of fools..."

"It hurts me, Lami. Mudi is now the so-called hero for helping a few of us get access to the urban nurses. He is being celebrated. The deal with the council of chiefs is beginning to yield dividends, while the real hero goes unsung."

Lami, excited, pulled her closer.

"Really?! Dividends?! Have you been able to access help? Tell me more, please."

"Ten of us were selected from Banza. The deal is that we will undergo ritual cleansing first before being allowed to go to the city. The nurses say we will have an operation called a vesicovaginal fistula treatment...it's a mouthful. These scarification marks are from the ritual cleansing ceremony."

"I am so excited. Finally! You will be visiting the big city; that is good, Halima, I am so happy for you... A solution for you and the others, at last. I can't wait for you to return," said Lami with tears in her eyes.

"Lami, we all know it was your idea. We owe our good fortune to your huge calamity. You are our benefactor. It has come at a high personal cost. Yet that bastard, my brother goes about town sowing his wild oats… I am so sorry."

Lami's smile faded and transformed to a frown.

"So, it is true? I heard the rumours, but I couldn't believe he would betray me in this way, sleeping around… the bastard!"

"Mudi is my brother and we both know this is out of character for him. I think he is so upset about losing you to his father. He is grieving by trying to replace your love with the lust for a thousand women. The loss of one's true love is difficult. The recovery is like putting together a shattered clay pot—it's never the same again."

Lami laughed hysterically, and for a brief second Halima was alarmed. She wondered whether her friend had lost her mind.

"Why do you laugh in this way? It scares me, Lami, it breaks my heart… seeing you this way breaks my heart."

"It's the irony of what you have just said and how far we still have to go to attain equality. My heart is also broken, isn't it? Just imagine that I respond to my heartbreak by sleeping with a thousand men? Would you or anyone still be so poetic? Would you or anyone be so sympathetic? You'd probably say, 'Hail the whore of Rolami, whose wares we have all seen being hawked on the streets of Rolami.' I would not be celebrated. Rather, there would be screaming, 'Rid this easy lay of her heartache for she desires a three-legged beast to bang her sorrows away.'"

Lami kept on laughing uncontrollably as Halima watched in horror.

"Woe to womanhood, they have made us a laughingstock. Even when we do an honourable thing they claim it as theirs.

When we succeed, they say they allowed it? When we scream for our rights they say we are uncultured and deserved to be homeschooled by sexual violence. When we feel threatened they say we brought it on ourselves. The worst part of it is that the leading voices in this stupidity are women themselves—"

"Lami, Lami, haba! I do not justify Mudi's actions and I would not. I understand what you are going through, and I do not say this lightly. I have been there before; was I not punished severely for speaking out and married off to a man I grew up calling Baba, a friend of my father? Did I not have to forgo the love of my life to marry the old man? I still bear the many scars of the torture meted out to me by the senior wives. They ganged up on me and beat me daily for being too vocal. Even his first wife, who was like my mother and named me at my birth, joined them,"

Halima whimpered. "This wrapper may look beautiful, but it covers many scars, and each scar tells a story of shame and despair. I lost a child, Lami, I lost a son and before I could grieve, I was labelled an outcast because my bladder leaked urine. I was cast to Banza, an abyss of darkness, a place for women they call cursed who all have the dreaded VVF. It was hell on earth, Lami. Che, the governor of Banza, forced several into servitude. We became ladies of the night for the very men who called us cursed. Men who said we were not deserving of living amongst our own people. This is the story of my life, Lami, our lives, but we must fight on and never think we are victims. We must celebrate the little victories because they coalesce into an immovable force. A force that may rescue generations of women yet to be born...I love you, Lami, and I thank you. Do not despair..."

They embraced. Halima was shocked by how emaciated Lami was, and they both shed tears.

Lami whispered,

"I wish you well in the city. I hope it all goes well, and you will have stories for me when you get back, my city lady."

Halima hugged her even more tightly and quietly said, "Thank you." They sat on the bed.

"Have you had breakfast? What will you eat? Mother will be so pleased to see you and even happier you are going to the city," Lami said.

"I am fine, dear, I saw your mother on my way in. Sit down and let me loosen this awful thing on your head! You must look presentable before I leave here today. And a warning: let me not hear you are living in the dark *o!* Unless...."

Halima spent the day with Lami, chatting like they were little girls again. Halima insisted Lami eat and they went through various beauty regimens. By the time Halima left, Lami looked different. There was a little sparkle in her eyes.

Lami lay on her bed that evening, smiling to herself. She was in better spirits. She whispered to herself,

"The battle is not yet over; it is still in its infancy. Women in Rolami will have freedom."

Her thoughts went to the plan that had been brewing at the back of her mind all day. The strategy of the widow, Riskatta, had given her an idea. She was excited and could not wait to share it with her gang of trusted friends. The full moon shone through her window, its rays caressing her cheeks as she closed her eyes to sleep. A new era may have begun in Rolami.

Chapter 11

Queen or Slave?
The Thousand-year Wait

Buzu had a quiet walk into the bushland with his personal bodyguards, two fierce-looking men armed with sharp daggers. It was a lovely Saturday morning. The lazy rays of the sun shone through the branches onto the footpath on which the fallen leaves had made a carpet. A cool breeze came through. It was beautiful and tranquil. Butterflies and other insects went about their usual business. The silence of the bush was only broken by the chirping of the birds.

Buzu walked through the bush, enjoying the beautiful scenery. He always felt like he was one with nature when he walked through this part of the bush. He had brought Mudi here often when Mudi was a boy and their relationship was cordial. He felt proud whenever he brought Mudi here and showed him various herbs and their uses along the way. Things had turned sour as Mudi got older. Mudi often said when they argued that he could not reconcile how being a man or "protecting manhood" translated to being a brute and a bully.

Buzu had been cross that Mudi kept Lami company and had warned him that Lami spelled trouble. He had threatened to disown Mudi but the boy would not listen to him. He felt very sad that his first son saw him as an enemy and had joined forces to campaign against him. He could not understand the reason for such hatred, but that was in the past now.

He swung his walking stick as he walked. Buzu had a morning ritual of picking fertility herbs for his potions. On this day, Buzu had the urge to answer the call of nature. He was unlikely to make it, as he was far away from his hut. During the hunting season, they had no choice but to engage in "bush gaming" (defecating in bush land). In the old days, a few young men engaged in this habit and went regularly into bush land for "bush gaming" even though they had toilets in their compound, claiming they derived some pleasure from this ritual.

The council of chiefs had been furious. In response, they put stringent measures in place to restrict this silly behaviour. Buzu told his bodyguards to be on the lookout and alert him if anyone was approaching. It would be embarrassing for a chief to be caught in this compromising position. Later that day, Buzu was getting married again to an unwilling and unlikely bride, Lami. He was pleased with himself. He had vanquished his sworn enemy Magda from the council and had now made his peace with his son and heir, Mudi. Marrying Lami was a bonus. All that was left was to dispose Goga on grounds of old age. A plot he had already set in motion with his allies and then he would be the chief of chiefs in Rolami. He would smoothly transition from being an elder in Rolami to become the chief of chiefs. He was a genius. He chuckled to himself.

At first, Buzu was suspicious of Mudi's motives, but his spies had since reassured him that Mudi was content with his position as chief. He was enjoying his new reputation as a modern reformer, thanks to the deal he struck with Buzu and the council. Mudi had also began to frequent Banza and had been seen with the "ladies of the night." This was much to the joy of Buzu and the disdain of Lami with whom he had not spoken since his elevation to chief. He'd heard that Lami was very bitter and disappointed with Mudi. It had even been said that she perceived Mudi's betrayal to be worse than marriage to his father.

How could she think he was a monster? After all, he had waited until her circumcision wounds had healed to set the wedding day. Buzu had boasted that he was going to make her cry tonight. He had promised that if the wedding sheets were not bloodstained, the whole town would know she was not a virgin. He would demand compensation for marrying her. Ideally, he would have asked that the dowry be returned but Magda had not taken the ceremonial dowry from him.

Stupid man, he thought to himself. *Having the nerve to say he was not selling his daughter.*

He wondered what was wrong with Magda; he seemed to have aged rapidly over the last few weeks. He had even offered to make a healing potion, which Magda refused.

The herb selection today was focused on increasing sexual stamina. This was in preparation for tonight. Buzu felt uncomfortable as his stomach grumbled. He walked quickly to find a good spot as he had begun to pass violent, foul-smelling wind. He started to whistle and sway, for he was a happy man, with the thoughts of the escapades of the night on his mind. Things could not have turned out better.

It was morning, and he hoped that there were fewer flies and the breeze was cooler. He was surprised to discover a few dry excrements on the path he chose. He cursed loudly. The council would deal with the idiots who continued to disobey its directives. He found a clean spot and positioned himself to begin emptying his bowels. He had only just started when he looked up to the sound of a breaking twig and saw Mudi and Unde.

He almost fell into his litter. "What are you doing here?"

"What are *you* doing here?" Mudi retorted.

"Isn't this against the law?"

"Mudi… you are not blind, and if you are, at least your nostrils are still able to perceive," Buzu snapped.

"This is a private moment. Leave at once with your crony. Whatever is bothering you can wait."

Buzu was so embarrassed, but at the same time relieved it was Mudi and not anyone else. He made a mental note to dismiss those useless bodyguards immediately.

"I am here to answer the call of nature," Mudi said, while Unde was holding back from bursting into laughter.

Buzu was covering his penis with one hand, while trying to prop himself up and maintain his balance with the other hand.

"Then look for your spot, son, and leave me in peace. You have not learned the etiquette of being a chief. You don't take your crony or bodyguard everywhere. They need to have boundaries…"

"Father, nature… nature is like the gods. How do we define it? It is an enigma? How can we fathom it?" Mudi smiled wryly.

"It sure looks after itself, it replenishes itself whether we like it or not, although we have our own part in keeping the cycle of life going. There is a time to be born, there is a time to die and then become part of nature, is that not nature, Father? I love it."

Buzu was quiet, reflecting on what Mudi had said. After a brief pause, his facial expression changed from disgust to horror.

"You called me 'Father'…you have not called me 'Father' in over five years, Mudi. Where are my guards?"

Buzu screamed, getting up quickly.

"They have answered the call of nature and become one with it. It came by the archer next to me. He is like the wind that cools you on a hot day and yet blows dust into your eyes. Be pleased they served you till the end…wasted life."

"You treacherous bastard…" Buzu growled. He looked around for anything he could lay his hands on.

"You are the king of treachery and I learned from the best," Mudi said. "How else could I beat you in your sick game, Buzu? You want to have Lami. I have coveted nothing in this life other than to wake up one day to have her by my side forever. I see her and the joy that wells within my heart restores my soul, it purifies me…"

"If this is about a woman, have her, she's yours."

"We have gone past that, Buzu. What has destroyed Rolami? Greed, the greed of a few men. What will bring peace? Simple. That our neighbours have peace and then we will be peaceful. I saw through your plans. I read you like a book, Buzu. You had your own selfish agenda. You made life hell for women, young people, the poor, the needy. You propagated lies in the name of customs, traditions, and the gods. Oh! The gods! They have not made one man greater than the other. Yes, the world is a theatre, some actors seem to have more important roles than others. Everyone is a lead actor in their own story because it is their story, Buzu… theirs! You have no right to change their story for your own selfish gain!"

"Do not do this for there will be blood…" Buzu pleaded.

"Of course, there will be blood! As we speak your cronies are all answering the call of nature, the final exit. Some peaceful, others not so. We need to replenish the earth."

Buzu trembled at Mudi's words, but tried valiantly to keep a brave face.

Unde, smirking at Buzu's nakedness, said,

"I am sorry to interrupt this father-and-son moment, but I cannot help but say that this was not the size of a penis I was expecting from a three-legged animal. It's barely bigger than my small toe…"

"It's the cold weather… It shrinks in cold weather…" Buzu stammered.

"…the size is affected by the weather…"

"Weather? You never stop to amaze me. So long, my father…"

"Don't be a coward…do it yourself…don't let your crony do your dirty work," Buzu said, desperation in his voice.

"Just following in your footsteps, my father. So long…"

Buzu screamed,

"You think there will be a new Rolami? You think all your men will be happy to see women tell them what to do and how to live their lives? You think the custodians will stand by and let you throw away our traditions and age-old rituals? It's your men that will fight you. It is their mothers that will refuse to heed your folly. All societies have their rites of passage and traditions. None is superior to the other, it's only different…"

"Well said,"

Mudi replied, clapping his hands sarcastically.

"You think you can deceive me? You forget that a culture that refuses to evolve becomes draconian and over time dies off! This revolution is not about overthrowing our customs and traditions. It's about removing those exploiting these traditions for their own selfish purpose. It's about making sure that our customs and traditions evolve with the times and remain relevant...."

In a flash, Buzu grabbed a short knife from his wrapper and dashed toward Mudi.

A brief struggle ensued, followed by a loud scream, then silence.

* * *

Hajaru had walked into Magda's room to invite him to come and have breakfast. She had prepared his favourite breakfast today. After all, it was Lami's wedding day. They had to try to make it special. A woman only gets married once in these parts. This was not the way they thought they would give her hand away in marriage. She had daydreamed about Lami's wedding. She and Mematha had spent hours planning Lami and Mudi's wedding over the years. All of that was now gone with the wind. She'd barely slept the night before, knowing that the day would be a very tough one for all. She had woken up early to make sure the *tuuwo shinkafa* was perfect.

A loud scream pierced through the morning. "Ahhhhhhhhhhhhhhhhhh!!!!! Nooooooo! Please, help meeeee!"

Everyone heard the scream. There was a brief commotion as everyone ran toward its direction. What could have happened? Had Hajaru hurt herself? Lajara was the first one to get there. She froze and let out another ear-piercing scream and fell to the ground rolling from one end to the other,

147

wailing. Lami, upon arriving at the scene, turned stone-cold and began screaming. "Noooooooo!"

She could not believe her eyes. Her father's lifeless body was hanging from the roof of his hut, suspended by her mother's favourite scarf. He could not bear to see his daughter married off to his enemy Buzu. The small note he left read:

"I love you so much and I will be with you to the very end, but this pain was too much to bear."

Hajaru was all curled up in the corner, weeping inconsolably, grabbing her head in her hands. Lami immediately sent for Danjah, her father's best friend. He could help cut down the body and plan for the purification of the room and the compound.

Magda's lifeless body lay on the bed in his room, dressed in his ceremonial dress. Hajaru stroked his face as tears streamed steadily down her cheeks. Lajara sobbed quietly, her arms around her mother's shoulders. Lami knelt beside the bed, her body laying over his, weeping bitterly.

"It's my fault," Lami muttered.

"I have brought this upon us. I am so sorry, why, Father, why?"

Danjah stood in the doorway, tears rolling down his face. He had sent messengers to Magda's family home to inform them. He had also informed the chief priest who would organise the cleansing ceremony. He wanted to give Hajaru and Lami some time to grieve in private. He needed their permission to send a delegation to Buzu's compound to inform them and call off the wedding. No wedding could be held today given the circumstances.

The mood was somber and slightly chaotic in Magda's compound. There were women everywhere wailing. The compound was filling with people as the news of Magda's death spread. Men were huddled in little groups, their heads bowed and arms across their chests. This was supposed to be Lami's wedding day.

Mudi and his men arrived at the chaotic scene. They were greeted by the news of Magda's demise, as everyone bowed in deference. Mudi made his way toward Magda's hut where his body lay. Lami saw him approach and got up, wiping away her tears, but to no avail. She was surprised at how angry she felt at the sight of him. She wondered why everyone was bowing to him and giving him so much respect. After all, he was only a member of the elders' council and not the chief of chiefs. With fire in her eyes, her voice croaky from crying, she yelled,

"What do you want!?"

Unde ordered everyone out of the hut except for Hajaru and Lajara. After they had all gone, Mudi was moved to tears, seeing Magda's lifeless body. This was the man he knew as father. Magda had taken him under his wings and been a father to him. He walked to Hajaru, bent down and held her hands. She was like his mother. She was his mother's best friend. He had spent hours with her as a little boy. She had provided shelter for his mother whenever Buzu beat her or threw her out. She had always been there for him. Hajaru stretched out her arms to Mudi, holding his hands for a few moments. Nobody said anything yet there were a thousand words expressed.

He turned to Lajara.

"Accept my condolences. He was like a father to me."

Lajara looked somber but nodded.

Lami watched him with her mother and her anger against him slowly faded. There was a special bond between Mudi and her mother. Mudi's mother had often remarked when they were younger that Mudi was the son Hajaru never had.

Lami asked again, this time in a more controlled tone.

"What do you want, Mudi? I have my father to bury and I have your father to marry, and saying both in one sentence makes me sick. It sounds like an abomination but that is what fate has bestowed on me…"

"I am sorry," he muttered. He walked toward her, extending his arms to her, but she stepped back as though his words repelled her.

Undeterred, he whispered,

"You asked what I want and all my life I have never wanted anything more than being with you, Lami, you complete me…"

Lami shook her head, visibly trembling.

"Go to your whores in Banza and all the harlotry spots. The damage your family has done to mine is enough, Mudi. You want me and then what, and there is a war because guess what, your father wants me, too…"

"Buzu is dead." "What…?"

"And so is Isti, Goga and all those three-legged creatures," Unde said.

"Before you stands our new chief of chiefs. He was pronounced the same by the chief priest a few moments ago. The coronation ceremony will take place later today."

"I came here to reinstate your father as the chief scribe only to meet a crowd informing me of his demise. I am deeply sorry,

Lami, I was counting on the wise counsel from you and your father. I love you, Lami, I always have, and I have not kept it a secret. It is common knowledge in Rolami. The change we desire in Rolami could not have happened by intellectualism alone. We were dealing with men set in their ways of treachery; to defeat them by chivalry is a pipe dream. I had to play their game to get them to trust me and then strike at a time they least expected. Your father…our father will have a state burial as a true reformer. I am saddened he will not be here to provide me with wise counsel. Together, we can challenge the custodians and stop the genital mutilations. We can educate the people, stop the violence, and most importantly, lead by example—"

"I want no part in this," Lami cut in.

"I did not hear you,"

Mudi said coldly.

"I do not want to be part of this," Lami said, louder this time.

Unde, who was already getting irritated, said,

"You cannot speak to the chief of chiefs that way. He has made his peace. If peace is not accepted, we give war—"

Lami screamed,

"I will speak to him as I wish. The door is open, go out the way you came in. I have my father to bury. I know you, Unde, you are a mule, and will put an arrow between my eyes if it pleases your master—"

"That's enough, Lami," Hajaru's voice cut in.

Hajaru immediately bowed, her face to the ground, signalling to Lajara to follow suit. They both paid homage to Mudi.

"Forgive her, my lord, your kind words are received with gladness. May you reign forever, Mudi. My daughter is tired, grief-stricken and perhaps delirious. What reasonable woman will hear your words and not leap for joy at the wisdom displayed by the great one? You called your action a game of treachery but my family and I see it as true chivalry. We are in mourning, but we are heartened that our father will receive an honourable burial. As we know, in our custom those who kill themselves are not buried amongst men of honour. Our daughter will be a worthy bride to the man she has worshipped all her life. A man who loves her. Leave it to me to teach her our ways while you attend to state matters."

Jorin, one of Mudi's cronies, hurriedly walked in. He bowed his head to acknowledge Hajaru and express his condolences. He turned to Mudi with urgency in his voice.

"My chief of chiefs, my sincere apologies. There is a revolt at the place of custodians and you are needed right away."

Jorin and Unde hurriedly excused themselves from Mudi's presence.

Mudi motioned to Hajaru and Lajara to get up. He looked directly at Hajaru.

"My mother, you have spoken wisely. I will leave now to quell this small revolt. I know that by the time I return this little girl will be transformed by your wisdom into a woman who is pragmatic, a wife who understands the slow wheels of change, and a mother who knows that the man of the house must do whatever it takes to protect his family."

Mudi began his slow walk toward the door. At the doorway, he paused, turned and looked at Lami squarely.

"You are my family, Lami."

She was still very angry with him for his visits to Banza. She was not moved by his speech, rolling her eyes and looking away, hissing and whispering under her breath.

"Family? Male prostitute."

Mudi took a quick glance at Hajaru before he quickly stepped out to march with his men.

Hajaru got up and walked toward Lami. She held her tenderly, putting her hands on her face and forcing her to look into her eyes.

Hajaru said,

"Lami, be wise, you never know who a man truly is until he has power. Mudi, despite becoming the chief of chiefs, with access to any eligible woman in Rolami, has chosen you. He has declared his love for you in public. You have known him all your life. You have desired to be his wife for many years. I am sure your father will be smiling down at this turn of events. Imagine all that you can do for women as the wife of the chief of chiefs."

Lami scoffed.

"It is better to live as a queen for one day than endure a thousand years as a slave to any man."

Lajara smiled wryly.

"You are now a queen, Lami, enjoy it while it lasts."

The End